This story is about Nirmala the Mud Blossom, who had the misfortune of being born female in Mumbai. Rejected and thrown into the dustbin when she was just two days old, the child was rescued and returned to her family by the NGOs.

Nirmala is ill-treated by her mother and subject to violence at her hands. She is allowed to continue her studies only because she can coach her younger brothers, as her parents are illiterate. On one occasion her mother brutally beats her when she is caught reading *David Copperfield* instead of doing the household chores; on another, she is struck for voicing her dreams of becoming a doctor. Loving school and the access it gives her to books she relishes, Nirmala accepts each beating with forbearance.

What will happen to this little mud blossom? Will she fight back or succumb? How can she rid herself of harassment and rise above the stigma she endures?

Nirmala: The Mud Blossom graphically depicts the travails, discrimination, and abuse faced by female children in India from the cradle to the grave.

NIRMALA

The Mud Blossom

NIRMALA
The Mud Blossom

Fiza Pathan

Fiza Pathan Publishing OPC Pvt. Ltd.
Mumbai, INDIA

Imprint: Freedom With Pluralism®
Publisher: Fiza Pathan Publishing OPC Private Limited
Symbol Apartments, Flat No 2, Tertullian Road,
Off Dr. Peter Dias Road, Bandra West, Mumbai 400 050, INDIA
Email: fizapathan@fizapathanpublishing.com
Website: www.fizapathanpublishing.ink

Book Layout ©2013 BookDesignTemplates.com
Edited by Susan Hughes, myindependenteditor.com, and Kimberly Catanzarite, www.editandproof.com
Cover Art: LLPix Photography& Design
Image: Sharvari Rane, licensed usage.

Book Title/ Author Name. NIRMALA: The Mud Blossom by Pathan, Fiza.
ISBN 978-8-1936044-0-3 Hardback
ISBN 978-8-1936044-1-0 Paperback
ISBN 978-8-1936044-2-7 Ebook

To the girl-child who suffers abuse from the cradle to the grave

And when Esau lifted up his eyes and saw the women and children, he said, "Who are these with you?" Jacob said, "The children whom God has graciously given your servant." GENESIS 33:5

–ESV

The belt came down hard on her back. She screamed as she tried to move away from her attacker, but the belt came down upon her again.

"You filthy witch, I'll teach you a lesson today," said her attacker, pelting the defenseless child again. The child was thirteen, but looked more like a ten-year-old. Tears rolled down her cheeks, and blood poured from a cut on her forehead. The child dragged herself to the corner of the hut near the place where the kitchen utensils were kept. It was not the first time her mother belted her, and she knew that it wouldn't be the last. She had become used to the daily beatings and the insults hurled against her. The belt hit her again, this time on her knee, the buckle opening a bloody slit where it sliced into her skin. This was her lot in life; she had no choice but to accept it.

The child's name was Nirmala, Nirmala Acharya. What crime had she committed to deserve a beating worthy of a convict in jail? She had been reading *David Copperfield* when she was supposed to have been washing the utensils and cleaning the hut.

"You dirty witch! I'll belt you to death," Nirmala's mother said as she whipped Nirmala one more time. After twenty lashes, Nirmala's mother, Tarabai, plopped herself upon a stool, panting with exhaustion. Nirmala, who was bleeding and badly bruised, lifted herself onto wobbly legs and stumbled to a steel container at the entrance of the hut. She poured some water into a tiny metal cup and handed the cup to her mother, who snatched it from her daughter's hands, raised it high, and drank. Tarabai handed the cup back to her daughter.

"Thanks, I needed that," she said, her voice tired. "And don't you go around reading books when you are supposed to be doing your chores, you hear me?"

"Yes, mother." Nirmala rinsed the steel cup and placed it in one of the niches in the mud and brick hut.

Nirmala Acharya was a resident of Mumbai in the country of India, a country of many diverse people, but also a place of poverty and struggle. Nirmala's hut was one among many that thronged the Bandra Reclamation area where hundreds of people lived in inhumane and unhygienic conditions. Nirmala was the eldest among four children. Her father, Ramesh Acharya, worked as a peon in a private clinic, while Tarabai, Nirmala's mother, worked as a domestic servant in middle-class homes. Nirmala had three younger brothers whom she looked after like a mother.

Nirmala poured water from a mud cup to rinse the blood from her wounds. She then sat on the floor of the hut and began to scrub the utensils with a cake of soap.

Her knee throbbed where the belt buckle had landed, but Nirmala dared not complain of the pain. She had learned very early in life that pain had only to be endured and never cured.

After slouching on the floor for a while, Tarabai went to the paanwala's shop, bought herself some paan, and returned to the hut, chewing the betel leaves with relish. Seeing that Nirmala was still washing the utensils, Tarabai kicked her in the stomach, making the poor girl squeal.

"So you've become lazy, you wretch. Hurry up with your work. Your brothers will be returning from school, and then you will have to take up their lessons." Tarabai growled, her lips red from chewing the paan.

Clutching her stomach, Nirmala wiped the sweat from her forehead with the back of her hand and continued to scrub the steel utensils in haste. When this chore was finally complete, Nirmala swept the tiny hut with an old broom . . . without complaining . . . without anger in her heart.

Three hours later, Nirmala's brothers returned from their afternoon school. They were hungry, so Tarabai cooked chapatis with some dhal and handed their plates to them. Nirmala was also hungry. She'd had nothing to eat since her school had ended at two p.m. After her brothers ate to their hearts' content, their leftovers were given to Nirmala to eat. The hungry Nirmala gobbled down the food. She always ate hastily lest her plate be pulled from her before she had enough.

After the meal, Nirmala washed the utensils once again and then, under the strict instructions of Tarabai, went to take up her younger brother's lessons. Nirmala taught her younger brothers with a gentle hand, even if they were troubling her. She loved her brothers and wanted them to do well in their studies. Mohan, who was eleven years old and the eldest brother, was smart and a diligent worker, the apple of Tarabai's eye. His notebooks were always complete and very neat, so Nirmala had no problem taking up his work. It was the other two brothers who were a problem. Mayur, who was ten, was a careless worker and hated to study, while eight-year-old Javed wouldn't sit in one place long enough to study.

Yet Nirmala dared not reprimand them, for if she did, she knew her mother would belt her or pull her hair in rage. Tarabai adored her sons.

After three hours of study and homework completion, Nirmala would help her mother cook dinner for the whole family. Their father would come back from work at eight o'clock every day and liked to see his dinner in front of him immediately—or he would belt Tarabai and Nirmala for slacking in their work. However, her father had nothing to complain about in this regard, as his food was always ready for him. Tarabai would serve her husband, then Nirmala served her brothers. The women did not eat until all the men of the house had eaten in full.

Ramesh Acharya earned one hundred rupees a day, which he entrusted to his wife each evening after he returned from work. In a month, he earned about three thousand rupees. Tarabai, on the other hand, earned a bit more from her domestic services at middle-class houses—about nine thousand rupees a month. Because they lived in a patriarchal society, Ramesh Acharya was treated like a god, while Tarabai served him dutifully. Nirmala watched all the proceedings with sadness in her eyes.

After dinner, her father went out to buy some betel leaves to chew, while Nirmala washed the dishes once again under her mother's supervision. The family then settled down on the mud floor and watched television, a tiny one placed at a height on a tall stool at the entrance of the hut. Nirmala, however, would not watch television but instead would leave the house and sit under the streetlight near the open drain of the shanties surrounding her, and there—away from her tortuous existence—she would study or read novels. The stench from the drains was overpowering, as was the odor of dried human excreta that surrounded the streetlights, but Nirmala was determined to remain very studious.

Passersby from the neighboring huts and shanties looked at her and proudly stated, "Nirmala, is so dedicated that she will certainly go the distance."

The truth was, Nirmala herself wished to do so: to go the distance. She wanted to get away from the hut and the beatings of her mother. Nirmala solved mathematical equations under the streetlight and then read the chapter in the English textbook that her teacher had just started that day. Nirmala wanted to memorize the full chapter so she would be able to answer all the questions pertaining to it in class and thus would impress her teacher.

Nirmala always impressed her teachers, for she was a first ranker and a brilliant child. They had often tried to get Nirmala enrolled in extracurricular activities, but she refused to take part in any of them, as she needed to return to the hut quickly to clean it and wash the utensils before her mother came back from work.

After studying a bit, Nirmala took her novel from her bag—*David Copperfield* by Charles Dickens—and began to read it. Her mother had almost torn the book that day in a rage, but Nirmala fought to keep it from her mother's hands and therefore was belted. The novel was a library copy, and Nirmala did not want the librarian to charge her a fine for damaging the book. Her parents already resented the little money they spent on her regular schoolbooks and fees.

As Nirmala leaned on the lamppost and read through the novel, she heard some shouting going on in a shanty opposite; the husband was pulling the wife's hair and beating her with a lathi. The shrill sound of the woman's screams echoed in the silence of the night, but Nirmala shut them out and concentrated on her novel.

*

"Didi, why does Ma call you darkie?" asked Mohan the next day when Nirmala was taking up his English meanings.

Nirmala looked at him with a smile on her face and said, "Because of my dark skin. Ma feels it is an ugly color, and I won't get a groom to marry me because of it."

Mohan tilted his head, pondering over her statement, and said, "I'm a darkie, too?"

Nirmala laughed heartily. "No, Mohan, you are fair by the grace of Lord Vishnu, so you will get a bride for yourself."

Mohan smiled at Nirmala, happy that he was not dark-skinned. "I'll beat up my wife just the way Baba beats up Ma," said Mohan as he slapped his imaginary bride in the air. Nirmala laughed again. "Mohan, my brother, if you do that, your bride will leave you and go back to her in-laws."

"But Baba beats Ma all the time, so why has she never gone back to her in-laws?"

Nirmala couldn't answer his question and so continued to take up his English meanings.

Ramesh Acharya came in early that day after work. When she saw the pleasant smile on her husband's face,

Tarabai inquired why he was so happy, to which he replied, "I got an extra tip at work today—five hundred rupees—and all because there were triplets born at the clinic."

Tarabai gasped in shocked as she held the money in her hands.

Ramesh said, "Use the money well, Tara, and buy some red bangles for yourself."

Nirmala was glad to see both her mother and father in good spirits that day. It was rare that her father got a tip at the clinic, and the whole family was jubilant. Dinner that night was a joyful celebration, with Tarabai and Nirmala serving the food.

Mohan then said, "Baba, can I buy some jalebis with the money?"

"Sure you can, beta," said his father with a smile on his face, "and Mayur can buy a new schoolbag, too."

Overjoyed, Mayur ran up to his father, put his arms around his neck, and kissed him with his dhal-covered lips. It was then that Nirmala remembered something. A book fair was going to be held in her morning school the following week, and the teachers had informed the students that Sudha Murthy's books would be sold at that fair. None of Sudha Murthy's books were available in the library, and Nirmala desperately wanted to read one. So gathering her courage, Nirmala, after pouring more dhal into Mohan's katori, stood before her father fiddling with the end of her dupatta. She said, "Baba, I . . . er . . . there is a book fair at our school next week so .

.. um ... I thought that if I could have some of the money to buy a Sudha Murthy book I would—"

Tarabai caught Nirmala by her long hair and pulled it hard.

"You witch!" Tarabai's screaming scared the younger children. "How dare you use your father's hard-earned money to buy yourself some worthless novels. Mohan, go and get my belt."

Mohan sheepishly picked up the belt from the niche his mother kept it in and handed it over to Tarabai. Nirmala's mother then whipped her on her back and arms. The shrieks of the child were heard by the neighbors, and many spectators came to the hut to watch her plight.

Red marks began to appear on Nirmala's body. Her knee wound, still swollen from the previous day's belting, began to throb in pain again. Nirmala lay on the mud ground in a fetal position with her fingers crossed over her head and her eyes closed tight. Their father motioned Mohan and Mayur to shut the door and windows of their tiny hut. The boys obeyed their father. Javed watched, dumbstruck, as his mother unleashed her wrath on his sister's body.

Nirmala's lip was cut, and her hair was matted in a bundle at the top of her head, bright red blood dripping from the mesh of her hair bundle onto the floor. All the while, her father did not rise from his position on the floor. He continued to eat his dinner and watch television, ignoring the screams of his daughter and the grunts of his exhausted wife.

Tarabai stopped belting her daughter after half an hour. Tired out, she sat heavily upon the ground next to her husband, fanning her red, sweaty face with the palm of her hand.

"Wretched girl," said Tarabai to no one in particular. "I would have stopped her schooling a long time ago if I'd known it would give her airs; however, I can't. The boys' education would suffer. I am uneducated, so I can't teach them."

Ramesh licked his fingers as he nodded his head in approval. "You are right, Tara. The only reason I send this girl to school is so she can teach her brothers. If I knew it would give her airs . . . why, I would have stopped her schooling a long time ago."

Tarabai nodded and then yawned loudly, staring at Nirmala, who still lay sobbing on the floor.

"Hey girl," ordered Tarabai, "get up now and wash the dishes, and I won't hear any more talk about buying books. Your schoolbooks are enough for you. And before you wash the dishes, clean up this blood on the floor. It's nauseating me."

Nirmala slowly rose to her feet. She put her hand to her head, and then looked at it. It was caked with blood. She wobbled to the steel container near the door and used a mud cup to pour water over her bleeding head. She licked her cut lips.

She could hear the whispers of her curious neighbors outside the house but gritted her teeth in anger. They were all the same. They had only come to see a tamasha—the entertainment provided as her mother beat her.

*

That night after her family was asleep, Nirmala slipped out of the house with her schoolbag and her *David Copperfield* novel. She was reeking of blood, and her knee was black and swollen from the beating. She threw her schoolbag on the ground, grabbed hold of the streetlight, and wept bitterly. Her sobs seemed to echo in the stillness of the night, but everyone was asleep in her neighborhood except a cat who was rummaging through the garbage bin for some food and a pack of pariah dogs who were roaming about.

Nirmala was in no mood to study. She felt as if her body was broken into countless pieces; the cold night chilled her until she shivered. As Nirmala sat, her back resting on the streetlight, she remembered what her mother's younger sister had told her when she was only five years old: Nirmala was basically the unwanted child. Tarabai and Ramesh Acharya wanted a boy to be born to them first, but it was not to be. Instead, Nirmala was born—the dark, weak, ugly daughter of their nightmares. Ramesh had tried to get rid of her, according to her aunt. He didn't want a dark-complexioned girl for a daughter, so one day after Tarabai had returned home from the hospital, he dumped the infant in a dustbin and returned home.

To their ill luck, they were found out, and Nirmala was returned to them by a group of NGO (nongovernmental organization) workers who had found the baby in the dustbin with the aid of some rag pickers. It was then that her father nicknamed his daughter mud blossom, for she had returned to them from the dirt of the city.

"Mud blossom," muttered Nirmala to herself over and over again until it sounded like another word entirely. A giant clot of blood had formed on Nirmala's head, which pained her terribly. She spat saliva onto her swollen black knee and rubbed the cool liquid over her kneecap. As she did this, she remembered how her aunt's words had hurt her to the core. She was an unwanted girl-child, a dark and ugly girl-child who would not get a marriage proposal.

"So what, mausi," said the five-year-old Nirmala to her aunt many years ago. "So what if I am a mud blossom? I'll go to school, become smart, and then work like a son to help Baba."

Her aunt laughed scornfully as she adjusted the dupatta of her saree over her head.

"My dear mud blossom, we girls can't be like sons to our families. We were born daughters and will remain daughters."

As she tenderly petted her wounded head, Nirmala remembered how similar her life was to that of David

Copperfield. Of course, he was the unwanted son, while she was the unwanted daughter. She laughed at that thought, wondering how a son could possibly be unwanted. Everyone in her family wanted only sons, not daughters.

Nirmala rested her throbbing head against the streetlight, picked up her book, and began studying the invasion of Babur into Hindustan.

*

Nirmala was a complete mess at school the next day. Her hair reeked of blood, and her uniform gave off an odor of excreta, as it had not been washed for a long time. All the students in her class complained of the stench, and even Nirmala's math teacher wrinkled her nose every time she passed Nirmala's desk.

"Hey, dirty girl, don't you have a bath?" asked a mischievous boy from the back bench, after which the whole class started laughing, and the math teacher had a hard time quieting them down.

Nirmala bore all the insults in silence, for she knew the truth of the matter was that she had just one uniform to wear to school, which could only be washed on weekends when school was closed. The previous weekend, however, Nirmala did not have the energy to wash her own uniform because of the belting from her mother. And Tarabai only washed her sons' uniforms, not Nirmala's.

Another boy from the back bench stood up in the middle of the class, and said with a malicious tone in his voice, "Don't you live in that Reclamation area in Bandra, Nirmala, where all the children do their potty on the streets? Well, did your uniform by any chance fall into that potty?"

The class roared with laughter, and the math teacher went to the back benches and scolded them. "You must not talk that way to any student," she said. "All children are equal in the eyes of God."

The boy who had made the comment about the potty said, "I don't mind treating everyone equally, but Nirmala always tends to stand out with her stench and filthy habits." Again, the class roared with laughter, and the math teacher hit the boy with her textbook.

Tears rolled down Nirmala's dirty face, the rivulets washing her cheeks clean. She wiped her tears with the back of her hand and continued to solve the math equation written on the blackboard.

Nirmala's family had a bath only once a week, due to the lack of water in their area. The politicians had made a promise in previous elections to build a public toilet and to ensure that fresh water would be piped to the people. After the elections, however, all promises were forgotten, as was always the case.

Nirmala solved the three equations on the board in a jiffy, as she was very good at math, it being her favorite subject. After the board work was complete, all the students got up to get their books corrected. When Nirmala got up to stand in the line, her grimy hair in a plait tied with an old red ribbon, the teacher looked up and twitched her nose at Nirmala, a signal to remain seated in her chair and she would pass by later to correct her work. Nirmala was dumbstruck; even her own teacher couldn't bear the stench of her body. And she was a first ranking student! But what was there to be done? Nirmala was filthy, so she sat back in her place, mortified by the teacher's attitude.

During the break time, the peons arrived in each class to provide weekly rations to the needy students whose annual income was below the poverty line, and Nirmala was one of them. Nirmala took three cartons of milk and a jute bag full of wheat grain and placed them near her desk. She then ate two vegetable sandwiches which were provided free for needy students.

Nirmala gobbled down the sandwiches like a squirrel, and then realized something: a drop of blood had fallen onto her desk. She put her hand to her head and realized that her head had started bleeding again. Avoiding further humiliation from her classmates, Nirmala ran off to the sickroom, where the nurse gently bandaged her head. The nurse was aghast when she saw the wound on Nirmala's head, but what could she do? Many such cases of abused children came walking to her sick room for free treatment, and she knew Nirmala was one of those students often belted by her mother or father.

"Do you want me to talk to your parents, Nirmala?" the nurse asked as she applied balm over Nirmala's swollen knee. "Or would you prefer the principal to do the talking?"

Nirmala shook her head. "I . . . er . . . I fell down on the road, and that's why I got these cuts. Don't inform my parents about anything, or they will beat me."

The nurse sighed sadly as she looked into Nirmala's eyes and saw fear written in them. Nirmala then excused herself and returned to class.

At least I won't stink of blood anymore.

When Nirmala returned home with the rations, Tarabai had not yet arrived, so Nirmala placed the huge bag of wheat grains at the side of the television and emptied the milk cartons one by one into a steel vessel and placed it on the ground. She then set about sweeping the floor, though it was a slow process due to the pain in her knee. When Tarabai arrived home, she was shocked to see Nirmala all bandaged up.

"Whom have you been telling about my belting you? Come on, confess or I'll kill you, you beastly girl," Tarabai said as she held her daughter by the throat.

"No one, Ma. No one."

"Then what about those bandages?" asked Tarabai.

"It was bleeding, Ma, so I had to stop it before anyone got . . . got . . ."

"Got what?"

"Got suspicious, Ma," murmured Nirmala in pain, choking out the words from beneath her mother's tight grip. Tarabai let go and left Nirmala alone to soothe her aching throat.

When Tarabai saw the rations her daughter had brought from school, she was pleased.

"Good job, my mud blossom, for getting us these rations. You can read your silly books now as a reward, or would you rather do something else?"

Seeing Tarabai in such a good mood, Nirmala said, "Can I go out and play with my friends on the road?"

"Go ahead, mud blossom," said Tarabai, opening the steel container of milk and smelling it for freshness. "Go ahead. You can play all day if you wish. I'll clean the vessels today."

Overjoyed, Nirmala changed from her school clothes into her red salwar kameez with a long dupatta and ran out of the hut. It was two in the afternoon, and the slum was bustling with activity. The foul odor from the drains blanketed the entire area. Some children made paper boats, placed them in the open gutter, and watched them float away. There were goat feces and vagabond dogs wherever one went. Housewives washed clothes outside their one-room huts, while groups of Muslim girls in their hijab passed by on their way home from school. Garbage was dumped in heaps all along the slum route, and adult men urinated near the rancid piles. Elderly gentlemen sat amidst the dirt and grime outside the mosque, chatting about the coming elections. Goats, sheep, pigs, and chickens ran amuck, paying no mind to the tiny naked boy who played in the middle of the road.

Nirmala walked on, past the paan shop, the butcher's shop, and the grain shop, waving gaily to all the slum dwellers as she made her way toward a hut behind the grain shop. She peeked inside to find a Muslim girl reading the Koran, dressed in her traditional black hijab and a light gray robe.

"Amina! Amina, I'm free today. Let's walk outside," said Nirmala. The Muslim girl lifted her head from the Koran and smiled at Nirmala. She then put a finger to her lips and shook her head.

"I can't come out today, Nirmala. Abbujaan is at home, and I've got to cook some mutton for him for his early dinner."

Nirmala's heart sank. It had been almost two weeks since she and Amina spent time together. Nirmala tiptoed into the tiny hut with the light green painted walls. She sat next to Amina and stared at the Koran.

"Can you really read that whole book?" asked Nirmala, fascinated by the Arabic handwriting.

"Yes, I can read the whole book, but alas, I can't understand a word of it." Amina closed the Koran and placed it reverently on a high stool just below the picture of the Kaaba.

"If you're willing to watch me cook, you can stay in the kitchen and talk while I clean the mutton chops."

"No way," said Nirmala as she backed out of the hut. "I've got one free day after a long time, and I'm definitely not going to spend it sitting in another dingy hut. I'm out of here!"

"As you wish," said Amina, getting up and removing her hijab, revealing her beautiful light brown hair. "Drop by tomorrow; then I'll be free."

"But I won't be free tomorrow," murmured Nirmala as she left.

Nirmala breathed in the filthy air as if it were filled with the scent of violets. She walked toward a garbage dump to chase the chickens with a stick. She ran after the hungry birds, singing a Bollywood song in a falsetto voice. Some of the younger slum children followed her with a smile, their naked bodies dirty and stinking, their laughter pure and sweet as they watched the chickens scuttle through the narrow, filthy lanes. Nirmala's bare feet splashed the gutter water onto the terrified chickens, and she forgot for a few moments all her pain, her anguish, and her wounds as she ran after the chickens without a care in the world.

An empty rickshaw was parked near the garbage heap at the side of the road. Nirmala and the naked children got into the rickshaw and pretended they were in a rocket heading toward the moon.

"Why is your head bandaged up?" asked one of the boys seated next to Nirmala. She tried to ignore the remark and pretended to be dialing some imaginary computer to launch the rickshaw rocket into space. However, one of the clever boys, Rihaan, who was sitting in the driver's seat, looked at Nirmala and said, "Her head is bandaged up because last night her mother belted her on the head. My father told me so when he came home from the factory."

"Forget your father," said Nirmala, raising herself from the rickshaw seat and climbing on top of the vehicle. "We are heading toward the moon like astronauts. Let's concentrate on that rather than my bandaged head."

The younger children teased her, so Nirmala left them and walked down through the rat-infested lanes of the slum. On her way, she came across a rather cute-looking white lamb tied to a pole near a Muslim's hut. She bent down and petted it gently, and the lamb nuzzled itself into her arms. She squatted down near the lamb and began to talk to it.

"You've got a luckier life than me, little lamb. The family that bought you will eat you sooner or later; whereas, I will be tortured till the day I die because I'm a dark-skinned mud blossom."

Nirmala stared at the lamb who bleated as it stood on its wobbly hind legs.

"So you want to play, do you? Little lamb, you have no clue that you're going to be someone's dinner soon. Then let's see how well you like it." The lamb bleated once again and scrambled down the lane.

Nirmala watched the traffic go by—people in rickshaws, taxis, fancy cars—they all seemed like people of another world, a world of which Nirmala had no clue. As the sun dipped below the horizon, men returned from their workplace, while the mosque sounded the azan.

Nirmala lifted herself up and stretched her limbs. A baby cried in one of the nearby huts. The wailing of the child and the call of the azan echoed in Nirmala's ears as she walked back to her home. Her mother was making tea when Nirmala entered the hut.

"It's about time you came back, mud blossom. Now go and bathe Javed. He hasn't had a bath for a week."

Nirmala obeyed her mother and grabbed her brother, who sat near the door, reciting his Hindi vowels, still dressed in his school uniform. Nirmala led him outside, carrying with her a tumbler of water, a round steel container, and a cake of soap. As she undressed him, Javed began to cry. He hated baths. Passersby looked on at the scene and sympathized with Nirmala, who was doing her best to keep him quiet.

"Javed, my little brother, don't cry. Your school friends won't sit with you if you don't have your bath. Please don't cry, Javed."

The boy's fidgeting had drenched her and his loud cries made it difficult for Nirmala to wash him. Hearing the commotion, Tarabai emerged from the hut, came toward Nirmala, and kicked her.

"You idiot, good-for-nothing girl! Can't you ever leave me in peace? Get back inside and get the tea ready for Baba and your brothers."

Nirmala, drenched and terribly cold, ran back into the hut and poured the tea into three petite glasses. Her father arrived home at his usual time. He put his daily wages in the box, tucked safely in the niche in the hut.

Nirmala offered her father tea, after which she served some to Mohan and Mayur. Ramesh was happy, as this time his tea had milk in it. Milk was an expensive commodity for the Acharya family, and so it was Nirmala's duty to bring milk to the house on ration day. Nirmala, however, never drank tea; she didn't care much for it, whether it had milk or not.

After serving her brothers their tea and getting them settled in front of the television to watch a Bollywood movie, Nirmala went back outside. She was greeted by Javed's cries as Tarabai struggled to finish his bath. Nirmala's red salwar kameez was wet, so she squeezed the lower part to drain the water from it and used what was left of the tumbler water to wash her legs and feet.

The sun had set, and a drunken brawl had erupted near Nirmala's hut.

"What's all that racket?" asked Ramesh, peeking out of the hut to get a look at the situation.

"What business is it of yours? Get back inside and get ready for dinner," Tarabai said as she wiped Javed dry with the end of her saree.

Ramesh shrugged and reentered the hut. Nirmala squatted down next to her mother and watched the angry men, five paces from her with spurious whiskey bottles in their hands, shouting at the top of their voices and threatening each other with dire consequences.

"Ha!" said Tarabai, pulling on her son's shorts. "Here we don't have money to drink a cup of decent milk, and there they are spending all they have worked for on the alcohol that ruins their homes. Ha! To hell with such people."

Nirmala nodded. "I'll never marry a drunkard, Ma."

Tarabai spat a wad of phlegm on the ground and declared, "You little witch, you will marry the person your Baba and I choose for you! Get me?"

"Yes, Ma," Nirmala whispered, though she knew in her heart that no matter what belting and abuse she had to endure, she would never marry a drunkard.

Nirmala finished her dinner early that night and placed a humble garland of jasmine flowers around the dirty image of Lord Vishnu in their hut. While the family was still watching the television, she slipped out of the hut with her schoolbag and returned to her streetlight. The drunkards had left, and the vendor shops were beginning to close for the night. Nirmala had borrowed a new book from the library after finishing *David Copperfield*. It was another book by Dickens called *A Tale of Two Cities*, and Nirmala was already in love with Sydney Carton, the lawyer.

"What a shame that he, too, is a drunkard," said Nirmala as she read the book.

She felt a sudden stab of pain in her right ankle. The book fell from her hands, and to her horror she saw a huge bandicoot, its razor-sharp teeth buried in her skin and tearing at her flesh.

"Oh, let go! Let go!" Nirmala screamed as she tried to hit the bandicoot with her fat book.

Tarabai, upon hearing Nirmala's cries, emerged from the hut at once and ran toward the street lamp, with Ramesh and Mohan on her heels.

"Let go!" Nirmala cried as the bandicoot tore a huge chunk of her skin and nibbled at it.

When Tarabai reached the scene and saw the tears in the girl's eyes, she asked, "What happened, Nirmala? What got to you?"

Nirmala shook her leg in an attempt to free the bandicoot, but it wouldn't budge. When Tarabai saw the creature, her screams mingled with those of her daughter.

Some of the slum dwellers heard Nirmala's cries and had come out of their shanties and huts to see what was happening. Amina, too, had emerged, wearing her black hijab and gray coat from that afternoon. Her father, Jaffar, upon seeing the bandicoot, rushed to kill it with a piece of glass, but Ramesh Acharya was quicker. Ramesh picked up a long, blade-like piece of glass, ran toward the filthy bandicoot, and stabbed it. Only then did the rat let go of Nirmala's ankle. It rolled onto its side, dead.

Amina ran toward Nirmala, patted her friend's head, and stared in horror at the wound on her ankle.

Jaffar looked up at one of the slum dwellers. "Come on, get a rickshaw ready. The girl will have to be taken to the hospital immediately. Get some rags to stop the blood, and Tarabai ... Tarabai ... Hey, Tarabai, what are you doing?"

Tarabai pushed Amina away from Nirmala, took off her slipper, and began to beat her daughter with it. "You wicked girl! Because of you, we will have to use up half our money on your hospital bill."

Nirmala gritted her teeth as Tarabai hurled abuse after abuse and spat on her. Ramesh Acharya stood by and shouted, "Hit her harder, Tara! Hit her harder! We've been giving in too much to her stupid whims and fancies; now let her learn her lesson."

Nirmala curled into a fetal position. "Why? I . . . I didn't do anything wrong."

"Who told you to sit out here alone at night when you have a proper shelter over your stupid head?" Tarabai said with a growl. "Now a rat has bitten you. Oh, if only it was a snake, I would have been rid of you at last."

Ramesh Acharya shouted, "Hit her, Tarabai. Hit her harder. She thinks that by studying under streetlights in the dead of night she will become a doctor. Hit her, Tarabai. Hit her!"

"Stop it, you two!" Jaffar stepped up and knocked the slipper out of Tarabai's hand. "She is bleeding profusely. She needs to be taken to the hospital. Where is that rickshaw now? Amina, hold on to her. She's shivering."

One of the slum dwellers readied his rickshaw to drive Nirmala to the nearest hospital. Ramesh carried the girl to the rickshaw. Mohan was left in charge of his younger brothers and watched as his mother and father rushed Nirmala into the rickshaw, which headed toward the hospital near their home.

CHAPTER TWO

Four years after the gruesome bandicoot incident, Nirmala, now sixteen years old, was sitting in her hut teaching Mohan about atoms and molecules. The boy, weak in science, paid little attention to Nirmala's lecture. He had grown fatter, with a pug nose and chubby fingers. Nirmala, on the other hand, had grown into a tall, beautiful girl with a slim figure, pretty features, and lovely tanned skin. She had just appeared for her tenth-grade exams and so was free in the evening to do her regular chores and teach her younger brothers.

Luck had favored Tarabai the past four years. She had started to work as a domestic servant in many more houses, including a posh house in Khar, and was now earning a monthly income of thirteen thousand rupees.

The only drawback was that she returned home later each day, just in time to cook dinner for her family.

Nirmala continued her efforts to make Mohan understand atoms and molecules, but the boy was more interested in playing outside with his friends. After a while, Nirmala gave into him, and Mohan gladly ran out of the house with the cricket bat his father had gifted him on his birthday. Nirmala closed the science book and placed it back in Mohan's schoolbag. She then sat in front of Mayur, who was struggling to solve a Bodmas sum in his book.

Over the past four years, all of Nirmala's brothers had become much less interested in their studies. Even Javed was becoming a handful where studies were concerned.

"Baba wants both of you to be make it big in life by going to college, getting a degree and then a good job," Nirmala said to Mayur and Javed. "How will you be able to do this at the rate you're going?"

Nirmala never laid her hands on the boys, for one complaint from them and her mother would belt her. Nirmala solved the Bodmas sum for Mayur, and after marking out some sums to do as practice, she got up from her place to do her sweeping.

Nirmala had finished giving her tenth-grade exams in March, and it was now June. Soon she would know her percentage, which then would determine which college she would attend. Her heart was set on becoming a doctor, and the best science college in Bandra was St.

Andrew's College. She hoped at least to touch a first class in her examinations. Amina, too, had given her tenth-grade exams, but she would not be going to college—her father had made sure of that. Nirmala felt sorry for her friend.

"Why is your father not sending you to college?" asked Nirmala one day when she caught Amina working alone in the hut.

"Abbujaan says I won't get a suitable groom if I go to college. He also says that since I'm past puberty, I should wear a complete burka and only cook in the kitchen."

"What's going to college got to do with finding a groom?" Nirmala tilted her beautiful head and watched while Amina kneaded the dough with both hands.

"I don't know. Something to do with custom, he says," said Amina, sweat forming on her forehead. "He says a woman should not be seen by any adult male, so I can't go to college because of that, even if I wear a burka."

"You could go to a girls' college, you know."

"He doesn't even want me to step out of the hut anymore, let alone go to a girls' college."

Nirmala remembered this conversation as she swept her hut. Amina had always wanted to work in government office, and she wanted to take up arts and study political science, but her father had dashed all her dreams against the walls of their one-room hut.

Nirmala vowed to finish her graduation, come what may. Until now, she had not discussed the topic with either of her parents, but she somehow felt certain that she would be allowed to go to college. Nirmala set the broom aside after sweeping the hut clean. She then lit sandalwood joss sticks before the image of the Lord Vishnu and prostrated herself before him. After that, she prepared a dinner of rice and curd while keeping a determined eye on her brothers. They might slack off, but she had no intention of doing so.

*

Nirmala followed Amina and her father to Shantaram's shanty, the only shanty in the slum that had a computer. Shantaram was an electrician by trade, as well as a matchmaker, and so was held in high regard by the people of the slum. When the threesome reached Shantaram's shanty, they saw that a large crowd of tenth-grade students already waited in line. The tenth-grade results had been declared, and the students crowded around Shantaram's shanty to see their marks, which had been posted on the Secondary and Higher Secondary School Certificate Board website.

Nirmala watched her friend Amina bite her lower lip as she waited in line for her marks. Amina was wearing a full-length black burka with a separate piece of cloth tied behind her head to cover her face across her nose and down her neck. Her otherwise slender figure was completely masked by this burka, which made

Nirmala—for the hundredth time—feel bad for her dear friend.

They waited in line for a long time. It was early afternoon, and the garbage bins surrounding the area emitted a nauseating smell. Shantaram's shanty was situated near a urinal, which over the years had turned into a mess hall for the dogs and cats of the area. The stench of excreta and urine weighed heavily in the air, but the slum dwellers were so used to it that they didn't even care anymore.

Nirmala waited, using her long green dupatta to constantly wipe the sweat from her face and forehead. She wondered how Amina could remain cool in the scorching heat, dressed in that black burka and uttering not a word of complaint.

Finally, it was Amina's turn to see her percentage on the computer. Shantaram sat in front of the computer, which stood in one corner of his shanty. He was a thin man with round, black glasses and a moustache that made him look like a Hindi professor rather than an electrician. He was dressed in his best kurta and dhoti, ready to aid all the slum children by looking up their results. He took a lot of pride in doing so.

"Amina bachchee, may the Goddess Saraswati bless you. What is your roll number?"

Amina whispered her roll number to Shantaram, who typed it into his computer. Amina wrung her hands fretfully, and Nirmala spotted her staring up at the heavens, perhaps begging for last-minute miracles.

Nirmala wiped the sweat from her brow with her dupatta, which by now was stinking with perspiration. Shantaram waited a few minutes for the computer to load, and then Amina's roll number appeared with her percentage below it.

"Sixty-eight percent! A first class, Amina bachchee," declared Shantaram, shaking her hands and patting her on the head. Amina's father was pleased as he stared at the percentage on the computer screen. He himself had never received an education, so he was happy that his daughter had at least passed her tenth-grade with a first class. This percentage would go well in getting her a proposal from a decent boy in the future.

"Next!" said Shantaram, motioning for the next person to step close to the computer. "Come on, Acharya bachchee. I don't have all day to wait, now do I?"

Nirmala adjusted her wet dupatta across her chest and neck as she stammered out her roll number to Shantaram. He typed the number on his computer; as Nirmala waited, she wished the ground would open up and swallow her. Soon her roll number appeared on the screen along with the percentage.

"Ninety-one percent, a distinction! Nirmala bachchee, you have outdone yourself. Congratulations on your great achievement."

Amina hugged Nirmala, and Amina's father gently patted Nirmala's head. Nirmala could not believe her good fortune; she was overjoyed.

Nirmala looked back on the past year, how she'd spent long nights under the streetlight solving one mathematical equation after another and practicing chemistry formulas. The beltings and abuse had continued along with the studies, but Nirmala was determined to get a good grade so she would be able to study at St. Andrew's College. Her hard work had borne fruit, and now was the time to celebrate.

Amina's father, generous by nature, bought both girls a box of sweetmeats from the vendor, and they gobbled them up with great joy. The girls giggled as they passed barefooted through the narrow by-lanes of the slum, gaily announcing their percentages. Not even the heat of the sun could dampen their spirits.

Nirmala's distinction was praised by all. To her pleasure, the butcher shop owner said, "So, Nirmala, we will be having a little doctor in our slum, eh?"

Nirmala blushed, grabbed Amina's hand, and ran out to the garbage dumping ground. They played with the street urchins amidst the debris and filthy garbage. While Amina and one of the urchins looked for Coca-Cola and Pepsi bottle caps in the floating mess, Nirmala sat with three urchins on her lap and told them stories about a witch called Baba Yaga.

"Hey, Nirmala!" cried Amina waving to her friend.

"What is it?" Nirmala picked lice from the hair of one of the urchins on her lap.

"Come and see for yourself," yelled Amina. "It's a used syringe."

Nirmala left the urchins and their lice, and rolled down from the summit of the garbage dump to where Amina was standing, still well clad in her burka. Amina was holding the syringe between her right thumb and index finger. Nirmala took it and let it rest in the palm of her filthy hand. The syringe probably belonged to one of the slum's drug addicts. Nirmala was aware that for drug addicts to lose a workable syringe was like committing suicide, but she had no mercy for the drug addict. She raised the syringe to the sky—the urchins and Amina stared at her in wonder.

"One day I shall become a doctor and will use such syringes for the good of mankind," Nirmala said in a thunderous voice.

The urchins in their filthy, bug-infested rags clapped their hands in delight as they followed the two girls down the lane, the syringe gripped tight in Nirmala's sweaty hand.

Nirmala's brothers were sitting in front of the television watching a cartoon when she entered the hut. Without disturbing them, Nirmala tucked the syringe in her geometry compass box. This was going to be her reminder for the rest of her life that she wanted to—would—become a doctor.

*

"So how much did you get in your exams?" asked Ramesh Acharya as he entered his hut that same evening. Mohan happily answered before Nirmala had a chance to speak.

"Didi got a distinction, ninety-one percent, and the highest in the school according to everyone."

Tarabai was cooking dinner in the corner of the house with the help of Nirmala, who boiled the rice with a smile on her face.

"Well done, mud blossom," said Ramesh as he sat on the mud floor. Then, without another word, he got up from his place and went to Nirmala . . . and patted her head. Nirmala hid her tears. This was the first time in her life that her father had patted her head. Many a time had Nirmala received blows and kicks from her father. His sudden kind touch choked her up, and a salty tear fell into the steel vessel of boiling water.

Ramesh then placed his daily wage of one hundred rupees into the box in the usual niche in the hut. Unbeknownst to his wife and sons, however, he smuggled out twenty rupees and handed it over to Nirmala. With a gushing smile, she pocketed it before Tarabai noticed.

Her father returned to his place on the mud floor, sitting next to his sons, who were waiting for their dinner.

"So now school is over for the mud blossom, Tarabai. What do you intend to do with her?" Ramesh said.

Instead of Tarabai giving the answer, however, Nirmala looked longingly toward her father and said, "College, Father. I want to go to college to earn a BSc degree and then go on to become a doctor. I've always wanted to become a doctor, Father."

Ramesh Acharya scratched his flea-bitten head. "College, you say, eh? Nirmala, my daughter, we don't have the money to put you through college."

"Don't worry, Father," Nirmala said as she sat crossed-legged in front of him, the boiling rice forgotten. "The government rule is that education for girls up to the twelfth-grade is free, and for later years, compensation will be given to a girl who wants to study further. Oh, do please let me finish my degree, Father! I . . . I'll die if I can't become a doctor!"

"Die if you must," said Tarabai who was cutting the cucumber. "But you are not going to any college."

The words fell on Nirmala's ears like hot coals. Her face went blank with dazed horror, and seeing her expression silenced the other members of her family. Tarabai continued to cut the cucumber stalk with her back to her children and husband.

"I've got no room in my house for lady doctors," Nirmala's mother said. "You will study only up to the twelfth-grade, get an office job, and earn for the family a decent amount until I get you a groom. No more talk of becoming a blasted doctor. We don't have that kind of money, and that's my final word on the topic."

The boys—including her father—sat dumbfounded. Nirmala, on the other hand, was panting, rage building inside her. Tarabai noticed this from the corner of her eye.

"Quiet, you mud blossom, or I'll belt you like the filthy dog you are and—"

Tarabai wasn't given enough time to complete her sentence, for Nirmala had picked up the belt from the niche in the wall and cracked it across her mother's arm. A torrent of bottled up anger and animosity led to a waterfall of emotion. Nirmala was older, stronger, taller, and bolder than before—bold enough to whip Tarabai.

Ramesh tried to push Nirmala away from her mother, but with one strike of the brass buckle, her father's head was wounded, and he lay down flat upon the muddy floor, screaming to his boys to get some help. Mohan was quick; he darted out of the hut, dodging everything in his path, and didn't stop until he reached Amina's house. Through tears and sobs, he explained what was happening in his hut, and soon Amina, her father, and two other slum dwellers headed across the road.

Amina, to her horror, saw Ramesh Acharya lying motionless on the ground, with Mayur and Javed crying above him. In the corner near the kitchen utensils, Nirmala hurled blow after blow on Tarabai's bulky body. Amina ran toward Nirmala. She grabbed hold of the belt, but after a short tussle, Nirmala regained control of the weapon and resumed her belting of Tarabai, screaming like a person who's having a fit.

Seeing Amina's helpless effort, Amina's father and another Muslim slum dweller grabbed Nirmala and squeezed her hand, making her drop the now-red belt. Nirmala, like one possessed by the devil, shrieked and wailed in the arms of Amina's father, who kept her from causing more harm.

Ramesh Acharya was rushed to a nearby hospital, while Tarabai was given water to drink, and Amina washed the wounds on her body. Neighbors flocked to the Acharya house, all of them saying the same thing: "The child has now taken her revenge."

Shantaram, however, did not come to the Acharya house to see a tamasha but to quell the rage of the same girl who had stood first in her class just a few hours ago. He entered the hut and saw Nirmala gnashing her teeth and screaming like a demon as she struggled to break free from Amina's father's arms.

Shantaram said, "Hey now, Nirmala, calm down right now, or the police will come to arrest you for man-slaughter."

Shantaram tried the best he could to calm her, but Nirmala spat out words of venom at her mother, accusing her of years of abuse. Still clad in her filthy, parrot-colored salwar kameez, now flecked with her mother's blood, Nirmala tried in vain to free herself from the clutches of Amina's father.

"Shantaram chaacha," wailed Amina, "please get Nirmala to stop, or she will hurt herself."

Shantaram spotted a pail of water near the door of the hut. He picked it up and threw the water at Nirmala. This one act quieted the girl at last. She lay in the arms of Amina's father, a faraway look upon her face. Shantaram wiped the sweat from his brow. The slum dwellers outside the house whispered to one another. Nirmala stared at her mother's battered body and the belt that lay on the wet floor, red with the fresh blood of Tarabai. She then cuddled up like a baby in the arms of Amina's father and went to sleep.

*

The next day, Nirmala's father was discharged from the hospital with a huge bandage around his head. Amina's father and Shantaram had gone to pick him up in a rickshaw. Her father was apprehensive about entering the hut, but Shantaram and Amina's father assured him that all was fine now.

As Ramesh entered the hut, his three boys ran to him and hugged him. Tarabai was slouched in the corner near the kitchen vessels, her body scarred with belt marks. Amina was reapplying an herbal balm on Tarabai's wounds. Nirmala was nowhere to be seen. This thought comforted Ramesh Acharya, who was now afraid of his daughter. Amina's father and Shantaram helped Ramesh Acharya to sit on the mud floor.

Meanwhile, Nirmala, in her same parrot-green salwar kameez, sat with two urchin boys atop a broken-down rickshaw that had been left to rot in the sun. The urchin boys played a game of nick-knack with their arms and feet, while Nirmala basked herself in the sun, not bothering to swat away the mosquitoes that swarmed from the open gutter nearby. Her face was swollen with mosquito bites, and the urchin boys began to tease her. Nirmala wished she'd just get dengue and die.

"Ha, ha, Didi! Your face looks like a juicy red tomato," said one of the boys while the other counted the bites on her pretty face. Nirmala allowed him to count them. She didn't care how she looked at that moment.

In the distance, a group of beggars were having an argument over a thousand-rupee note they'd found lying in the mud. Alongside them, MCGM workers with masks on their faces were sweeping the road.

"Guess they can't tolerate the stench, eh?" said one of the urchins as he scratched his gritty face.

"This is the stench of Mumbai," said the other urchin, "and slums are the face of Mumbai. They best learn how to live with it."

Nirmala said nothing. Her geometry box was clutched tightly in her hand. She winced as a mosquito bit her on the lip.

It was Shantaram who found her later on and brought her to the hut. Both Ramesh and Tarabai stared at her warily with a look of fright upon their faces. Nirmala clutched her geometry box to her chest and said nothing. When the silent communication became too much, Shantaram ventured to break the ice.

"Oye, Nirmala bachchee, let bygones be bygones now. Ramesh bhai has learnt his mistake and so has Tarabai. Let's all forget this episode and become one happy family again."

When Shantaram realized that no one was making a move to speak, he pulled up his sleeves nervously, looking from Nirmala's face to her father's. He knew that if he was not careful with his words, the next person to be belted would be him. So after thinking for a while, Shantaram motioned for Nirmala to sit down near her mother. Amina smiled at Nirmala, which meant more to Nirmala than Shantaram's hollow courtesies. Nirmala took the cheap herbal balm from Amina's hands and began to apply it to her mother's wounds. With her free hand, Nirmala placed her geometry box and its precious syringe into a box near the salt tumbler. Tears welled up in Tarabai's eyes, and she brushed them off with the end of her saree.

"I want to say something to everyone," Nirmala said as she continued to rub the balm onto her mother's wounded skin.

Everyone looked up at Nirmala's mosquito-bitten face, their eyes encouraging her to continue. Amina sat crossed-legged in her burka, leaning against the red gas cylinder.

Nirmala continued. "For my whole life, I have lived like a slave to my family. I've been beaten like a dog and treated worse than a stray rat from the slums. Yet I bore it all with one aim and one aim alone—that one day I would become a doctor and serve humanity. However, here again, I am to be overruled. My family does not wish me to become a doctor, for they cannot afford it. They cannot afford me anything, not even my one and only wish."

Here Nirmala started to cry, and Amina came close to gather her in her arms, but Nirmala stopped her.

"I've always been the mud blossom of this house. I was taken from dirt, I live in dirt . . . I am dirt! So I've decided for myself that I'm . . . I'm going to finish . . . finish my twelfth-grade and get a decent office job, just as Ma and Baba wish. Maybe my sacrifice today will forgive the sins of last night's behavior, and maybe some-day—in my next birth—I will become a doctor."

Ramesh Acharya held his wounded head low, and Tarabai sobbed loud enough for everyone to hear.

*

Two years of junior college passed like a whiff of gar-bage in a moving garbage truck. It was painful, yet it was for the good of all. Nirmala never again tried to belt or hit her father or mother after that day. Her parents grew to respect her, though in a sort of terrified way. They rarely spoke to her.

As expected, Amina was not sent to college. She was made to stay at home and learn how to cook from her aged grandmother. She rarely came out of her home, and whenever she did, she was always covered from head-to-toe in a black burka. Her face, too, was masked and her eyes were hidden behind a swath of mesh stitched into the hijab or headdress of the burka.

Nirmala gave up the idea of taking science as her stream of study in college. Instead, she took up arts. She did this so the material to be studied would be easy, leaving her plenty of time to teach her younger brothers. Nirmala studied subjects like history, psychology, economics, sociology, English and Hindi in her college library. As she studied at St. Andrew's College, she felt blessed that she was destined to study at the college of her dreams. So what if she was not to complete her graduation; at least she was learning and growing intellectually, and that was more important to her.

At St. Andrew's, everyone in her class called her Chili, because she only wore two kinds of salwar kameez to class: a green one and a red one. Many of the girls would not sit next to her because her clothes emitted a stench of sweat. Yet even here, God was merciful to Nirmala, and she made two good friends, the studious Ameera Sheikh and the naughty Neil Perez. The three friends often sat together in the library and studied and ate together at the college canteen, talking about the latest gossip.

"Hey, you know what? Andrea Mascarenhas is going out with Paul D'Souza," Neil Perez said, winking at Nirmala and Ameera.

"No way," Ameera said. "That's the third person she's gone out with since she started college."

"And knowing Andrea, it won't be the last," Neil said, and the three of them laughed out loud, drinking their coffee and eating samosas from the canteen.

Ameera would often tease Nirmala about Neil when he was not around. Nirmala didn't like that at all, although she liked Neil as a friend.

"How can you say such things about Neil and me?" Nirmala was wearing her trademark red salwar kameez while they strolled through the campus corridors.

"I know he likes you." Ameera giggled. "It's so obvious. Everyone else in class can see it—everyone but you. Even in the library, he constantly stares at you with an affectionate gaze. Face it, Nirmala, you are such a bookworm that you haven't even noticed Neil."

Nirmala had morning college and returned home every day at around one o'clock in the afternoon. Being the first one in the hut, she would sweep the floor, cook the rice and curd for her brothers (who would arrive from school after four o'clock) and then go to the vegetable vendor to buy cucumbers and carrots for dinner. After having done all her chores, Nirmala would go to Amina's house to spend time with her, watching her cook food for her father. Before returning home, she played with the urchins of the slums near the garbage dump. More than playing with them, Nirmala would sift through the garbage and fish out various items like pen refills, notebook spines, a half-full packet of Uncle Chips, an old pouch, Hamilton-bound used notebooks, and other useful treasures. She would then distribute these items to the urchins and keep a few precious ones for herself.

Amina often told her to avoid rummaging in the filthy garbage with the urchins, as it made Nirmala stink, but Nirmala ignored her words of wisdom.

"I'm a mud blossom, and the mud is my home. I was not born from my mother, but from the dustbin."

One day, however, Nirmala saw something that scarred her for the rest of her life. After haggling with the vegetable vendor, she and a group of urchins were searching for iron tins in the garbage bins. They searched for half an hour but could not find anything, till at last one of the little girls stated that she had found something strange in one of the dustbins.

Nirmala left the slimy plastic bag she'd been investigating and walked over to the little girl. Nirmala shook the dustbin, as she couldn't see at first what the girl had found. Then she put her hands into the dustbin and yanked out a pair of tiny bones.

"What is it, Didi? Tell us! What is it?" The urchins prattled on whilst Nirmala turned green in the face. She dumped the bones inside the dustbin, ran to the other side of the garbage dump, and began to retch. The strands of hair around Nirmala's face were soon drenched in vomit, and her eyes brimmed with tears.

After dinner, while Tarabai was chewing betel leaves and Nirmala was taking up her brother's schoolwork, Ramesh noticed the smell of vomit in the air and asked the family who it was that had vomited and not washed up. Nirmala hung her head and nodded, which made her father anxious.

"Are you in trouble?" he asked, worry written all over his face. Nirmala cackled like a crazy woman, and tears rolled down her face. Of all the things to worry about, her father thought she was pregnant. When she finally stopped laughing, Nirmala wiped her eyes and took a deep breath.

"Don't worry, Baba. I'm not one to give anyone trouble but myself. I had to vomit; anyone would vomit to see the dead remains of a fetus in a dustbin. Guess that baby wasn't as lucky as I was, huh?"

Tarabai spat out her betel juice, and a tear ran down her cheek.

"Must you dig into all the dustbins of the slums and hurt our hearts so?" Tarabai wailed, which made the three younger boys bow their heads in shame. "And, yes, if it were in our hands, we too would have ended your life, like the fetus you saw in the dustbin. But we would not have done it because we hate you, but because a woman's life in India is a pain hard to bear. Become a wife with children one day, in your in-laws house, and you'll see the real meaning of the word hell."

Nirmala went to Tarabai and put her head on her mother's shoulder. Tarabai's tears trickled down and dripped onto Nirmala's cheek, washing her face clean of the vomit. Ramesh Acharya, his body wrecked with age, struggled up from his place and stood before the image of the god Vishnu. He prayed aloud:

"O my god, please be merciful and give us the blessing of a son-in-law who will not hate women. Please,

Lord Vishnu, please turn the tears of girls into smiles, reach out to us in our time of need. Reach out to us . . . reach out . . ."

*

Shantaram entered Nirmala's hut one Sunday afternoon. Tarabai was there to greet him alone. Ramesh Acharya had taken his son, Mayur, to a local playground to watch some cricket for free while the other boys and Nirmala were out roaming about the slum in the heat of the noonday sun.

"Sit down, Shantaramji," said Tarabai. "Would you like to have some sugar biscuits or maybe some chai?"

"No, don't trouble yourself, dear lady," Shantaram said as he made himself comfortable on the muddy floor.

"No trouble at all, sir. After all, you have come with some good news to serve our purposes."

After a lot of coaxing, Shantaram had a glass of strong tea and some cheap sugar biscuits. Tarabai also offered him some betel leaves to chew, but he refused the offer, so Tarabai ate the betel leaves herself.

"So, Shantaramji, what is the news? Have you brought any proposals for my daughter?"

Shantaram took a last sip of his tea and, after wiping his mouth with his sleeve, pulled a bundle of photographs from his jhola and spread them on the floor. Tarabai smiled as she perused the many photographs of young men placed in front of her.

"Are they really all wanting to marry my little mud blossom?" asked Tarabai.

"Indeed, madamji. The good qualities of your mud blossom have reached the ear of many families. Also her being only a twelfth-grade appeals to many families, for they feel that girls who are graduates and postgraduates have many airs. By the grace of god Shiva and his consort Parvati, our Nirmala is only a twelfth-grade. Also, she is at the ripe age of eighteen—a very good age to settle down in life with a man of her liking."

Tarabai spat her betel juice into a copper container and picked up each photograph. She had many questions about each of the young men.

"They do know that we are poor and can't pay a large dowry for the marriage? The marriage itself will have to take place on a small scale because of our budget."

"You leave all that to me," said Shantaram, tapping his chest. "Nirmala bachchee resides here in my heart. Tarabai, all will be taken care of. You just choose the man."

Shantaram went on with his work, describing to Tarabai the qualities and qualifications of each candidate who had sent his picture. Their conversation went on into the latter part of the afternoon. Tarabai was not really concerned about the looks or the qualifications of any of the men, so long as they had a job, a roof over their head, and would not express their wishes for a large dowry.

By five o'clock that evening, Tarabai had found only one proposal she liked, that of a young man called Dheeraj Manoharan. The boy lived in a two-room apartment overlooking the largest slum in Dharavi. He lived there with his mother, father, and grandfather. The father was still working at a factory, the mother was a housewife, and the grandfather was a retired school teacher. Dheeraj Manoharan himself was working for Tata Consultancy Services as a consultant. He was a graduate and earned twenty thousand rupees every month. Tarabai was also glad to know that the family had asked for a dowry of ten thousand rupees, which Ramesh Acharya could afford. The boy himself looked decent, fairer than Nirmala the mud blossom, but Nirmala had better features.

"So what do you say, Tarabai?" Shantaram was tired from the long day of negotiations. "Do you want me to send Nirmala's horoscope to this family?"

Tarabai nodded, still staring at the picture of Dheeraj Manoharan.

Shantaram gathered the other pictures together and put them in his jhola. With a salaam, he left the hut.

*

You're getting married?" Ameera Sheikh's loud squeal startled the couple kissing in front of them.

Nirmala and Ameera were seated on the steps of the main lecture hall as students scurried up and down around them. When Nirmala told Ameera that she was to get married by the next week, Ameera was stunned, almost dropping the giant Anthony Giddens Sociology textbook from her hands.

"But . . . but what about your graduation?" Ameera said.

Nirmala, in her red salwar kameez, gave a half smile and said, "It was a deal I made with my parents. I was to finish my twelfth-grade only, get a decent job, and then get married."

Ameera blasted Nirmala with various points of objection, but Nirmala just stared in wistful silence at the couple in front of them, locked in a passionate kiss.

Their twelfth-grade exams were just over, yet Nirmala had not found a decent job. She explained to Ameera that she would find one after marriage, as her in-laws were not against a daughter-in-law working after marriage. When Ameera again pestered Nirmala about her graduation, Nirmala stated that she would complete her graduation in her next birth.

"I don't believe in rebirth," declared Ameera. The annoyed expression on her face made her look cute in her black hijab.

The couple was still kissing, and Nirmala still had a deadpan look on her face. Ameera scowled at the couple.

"And what about Neil?"

"What about him?" whispered Nirmala.

"He loves you and wants to marry you after he graduates and gets a job as a photographer."

"Who said so?"

"Everything in this world need not be written in textbooks, Nirmala. These are feelings which need to be felt. I've seen the way he looks at you. Don't tell me that he, too, will have to wait till your next birth?"

Nirmala stood, her Modern Contemporary History book still in her hand. The couple got up and walked arm in arm toward their class.

"Let's return our books to the library," a solemn-looking Nirmala said. "We won't be needing them anymore . . . at least not me."

Nirmala's wedding was a quiet one. The bride and bridegroom did not meet each other at all before the wedding, as the boy's parents did not approve of it. Tarabai saw to the mandap—the wedding altar—decorations, as well as the lights. She also used her own money to buy Nirmala some new salwar kameez to wear in her in-laws house. Ramesh Acharya provided a live band to play on the wedding day. Only a select few of the slum dwellers were invited for the wedding, which caused a lot of ill feeling afterward, for Nirmala was a friend to almost everyone in the Bandra Reclamation slum.

On her wedding day, Nirmala dressed in a dark red saree with a cheap golden border. She was bathed by Tarabai and Amina on the morning of the wedding. During the wedding ceremony, Nirmala did not even look up to see the face of the groom. The Hindu temple priest chanted mantra after mantra throughout the ceremony.

Ameera came to the wedding clad in a very shiny purple embroidered salwar kameez, with her dupatta

covering her forehead. Neil did not come but sent orchids with Ameera, which were handed over to Nirmala
when the kanyadaan—a ceremony where the girl is of-
ficially gifted to the groom by her father—was over.
Shantaram ate a lot at the wedding, while Amina's father hid his tears, lest they be seen by Amina—hidden
in her head-to-toe beige burka—as she aided Tarabai
throughout the ceremony.

At the end of the wedding, Nirmala was escorted to
a taxi where her groom was waiting to take her to their
home in Dharavi. Tarabai wept and so did Ramesh
Acharya. Nirmala's brothers hugged her, rumpling her
bridal gown. Nirmala, however, did not shed a single
tear and spoke not a word throughout the ceremony.
With Neil's orchids in her hand and her old geometry
box tucked under her arm, the syringe still inside,
Nirmala gracefully entered the taxi, and the door closed
shut behind her.

CHAPTER THREE

Her in-laws greeted Nirmala warmly in her new home. Her husband, Dheeraj Manoharan, was a shy man, and even though Nirmala did not love him, she grew to respect him. Dheeraj Manoharan was also a prayerful man. He was the first to rise each day, and, after a cold bath, he would spend an hour before the gods in the puja room, chanting prayer after prayer. Only then would he sit down in his office clothes to eat the breakfast Nirmala had prepared.

Nirmala learned the ways of the house easily. She got up early every morning, prepared the breakfast and tea for the entire household, and then took her bath after her husband, as they had only one small bathroom in the house. Nirmala wore jasmine in her hair and a big red bindi as she went about her household chores. Her mother-in-law, Kesaribai, handed all responsibility for the house to Nirmala but also encouraged her to look for a job.

"Can I give half my earnings to my mother?" asked Nirmala one day as she searched for an appropriate job in the classified section of the *Times of India.*

"By all means. You have every right to do so," said Kesaribai, sitting on the floor of the hall with her rudraksha (a rosary) in her hand, chanting the name of Ram.

It took three months, but at last Nirmala secured the job of a preschool teacher at one of the Dharavi slum's preschools for poor children. Since she had not done her teacher's training course nor her graduation, she was paid a salary of only nine thousand rupees, half of which she gave to her mother when she visited her once a month to inquire about her brothers. The other half she placed in the hands of her mother-in-law, Kesaribai. Nirmala left for work after her husband and father-in-law, Soham Manoharan, left for their jobs. She returned home in the afternoon around two o'clock and prepared lunch for Kesaribai and the patriarchal grandfather, who spent his days praying, reading the newspaper, and staring out the window, observing the activities of the Dharavi slum dwellers.

Nirmala then swept and mopped the house and washed the clothes in the bathroom. Soham Manoharan was the next person to return home from the factory, and it was Nirmala who gave him his black coffee and chapati, an unleavened wheat bread. Dheeraj returned home around eight o'clock in the evening. Nirmala touched his feet and received his blessing and then served him some bread and butter and his special coffee with three teaspoons of sugar in it. Husband and wife then sat at the dining table and spoke about whatever came to mind: work, salaries, the neighbors, dinner, news, and many other topics.

Nirmala enjoyed her job as a preschool teacher and slowly began to enjoy her life as the wife of Dheeraj Manoharan. Ameera would call once in a while to inquire about her health. Neil Perez didn't call at all, but sent news about himself via Ameera. Everything seemed lovely, and Nirmala thought her life as the mud blossom would soon be over. She could not have been more wrong.

*

Shantaram was fixing a study table lamp with the help of his assistant when Tarabai entered the workhouse part of his shanty. She was beaming and offered Shantaram a peda from a box of sweetmeats she carried in her hand. Shantaram took one and smiled.

"So, Tarabai, what is the good news? Has your eldest son stood first in the class?"

"No, you silly boy. It's my mud blossom."

"Ah, our dear mud blossom." Shantaram sighed, motioning for the assistant to continue working. "The slum seems so empty since Nirmala left. It's not the same without her beautiful, dusky face. What news about her, Tarabai?"

"The best news possible, Shantaram. By the blessing of the Triune head Brahma, Vishnu, and Mahesh . . . Nirmala is with child!"

Shantaram gasped. "You . . . you mean our Nirmala is pregnant? Our mud blossom is with child? Oh Tarabai! This is the best news I have ever heard!" Shantaram ran out the door and shouted the good news to his neighbors. "Are sunte ho—listen everybody! Hear the good news of the season. Our mud blossom Nirmala is with child! Spread the good news; Tarabai is going to be a grandmother!"

Indeed, Nirmala was pregnant, and the slum dwellers at Reclamation were not the only people who were delighted by the news; her in-laws relished the joy of the new arrival into the Manoharan family. Dheeraj Manoharan treated all his co-workers to a splendid Gujarati thali, while the patriarch who was soon going to be a great-grandfather called all his old colleagues to tell them the good news. Kesaribai was ecstatic. She hugged Nirmala again and again, and kissed her forehead, smudging the bindi. Ameera Shaikh, who was doing her first year B.A., visited Nirmala's in-laws' residence with a huge, well-decorated bouquet of flowers.

"Ameera, dearest," exclaimed Nirmala as she took the bouquet from Ameera's hands, "there was no need to spend so much money."

Ameera laughed aloud. "Nirmala! Oh Nirmala, this bouquet is not my present to you. This bouquet is from Neil. I'm just the delivery girl."

Nirmala gazed with affection at the bouquet of jasmine, red roses, lilies, and blue orchids, and then she invited Ameera for tea.

That night, when her husband finished reading his Hanuman Chalisa and Nirmala had finished her chores for the day, they sat on their bed—the only bed in the house, placed in the privacy of the married couple's bedroom—and Dheeraj Manoharan kissed Nirmala on the cheek.

"Thank you so much for such a wonderful gift, Nirmala."

Nirmala blushed and lay down on the bed, tired yet happy.

However, Dheeraj Manoharan had not yet finished talking. He leaned back on the bed, both hands behind his head.

"I've so many dreams for our son, Nirmala. He will become a great person and will continue the name and pride of our family. Our son won't be just a consultant like me or a preschool teacher like you. Certainly not. He will be Lord Shiva's gift to us and our family."

Nirmala giggled and turned toward her husband. "But Manoharanji, suppose your son turns out to be a girl. Then she will be Goddess Parvati's gift to us, won't she?"

Dheeraj Manoharan clicked his tongue and stared off into the distance. "No, Nirmala, the child will be a boy."

Again, Nirmala giggled innocently. "How can you be so sure, Manoharanji? I have a feeling—mother's instinct, let's say—that the child will be a girl. We will dress her like a doll with pretty dresses and—"

"What I've said, I've said, Nirmala. Do not contradict. The child will be a boy! Only a boy."

"But how can you—"

"No buts," said Nirmala's husband. "The child is a boy; the Lord Shiva has promised me. I've not been praying to him for nuts. The child will be a boy. Now, let's sleep. I have a busy day at the office tomorrow. Good night, Nirmala."

"Good . . . good night, Manoharanji," Nirmala whispered, still in shock. She turned over, puzzled. A chill ran up her spine and her lips began to quiver. After a while, she shook her head and smiled to herself. Perhaps it was just her husband's fancy for a boy that made him say those words to her. Her husband was not like her parents; he would accept either girl or boy when the time came. He was different . . . wasn't he?"

*

In the month of June, when the monsoon reigned supreme in the city of Mumbai and the gutters overflowed throughout the slums, disrupting traffic and flooding the shanties, Nirmala's child was born. Her labor pains began on the nineteenth of June, and her in-laws rushed her to the government hospital.

It is a custom in India that a pregnant woman should spend the last three months of pregnancy in her mother's house; however, due to lack of space and proper sanitary conditions, Nirmala's mother-in-law decided that Nirmala would stay in her husband's house for the whole pregnancy. Ramesh Acharya and Tarabai agreed with Kesaribai's wishes, as they felt she was a wise woman.

On the nineteenth of June at 11:15 a.m., Nirmala was taken into the labor room. Dheeraj's father, Soham Manoharan, called him to the hospital. He arrived while Nirmala was still in labor. Tarabai came to the hospital with Mohan, worry shadowing her face. Trailing behind her came Shantaram, with his customary jhola. It was he who played the calming force amidst the chaos, instructing everyone present to trust in the abilities of the attending doctors and to pray to the Lord Ram, the vanquisher of Ravana, for all to go well. Following this advice, everyone sat or stood around the ward, chanting the god's name. Ramesh Acharya had remained at the hut to care for his younger sons, but Shantaram used his old, cheap Nokia mobile phone to keep him informed of all the happenings in the hospital.

After eight hours of labor, Dheeraj Manoharan at last heard the sound of an infant's cry. Everyone outside the labor room yelled in joyous unison, and none was louder than the excited matchmaker and electrician, Shantaram.

"My Nirmala bachchee is a mother today! Suna Tara-bai—did you hear that? —the child is born. You are a grandmother!" Then screaming into his mobile phone, Shantaram almost made Nirmala's father deaf as he clamored about the birth.

Dheeraj Manoharan went down on his knees with his hands joined together, thanking all the gods for their blessings. Half an hour later, a pudgy nurse came out of the labor room with a baby in her arms, followed by the doctor.

"Congratulations, Mr. Dheeraj Manoharan," said the gynecologist as he rushed downstairs.

The nurse raised the baby and said, "Very healthy baby, sirs, and the mother is also doing fine. The baby weighs eight pounds."

Dheeraj Manoharan grabbed the baby from the nurse. Caressing it with tears in his eyes, he exclaimed. "Lord Shiva, the most holy of sages, has kept his word. My son is born today!"

The nurse chuckled at Dheeraj Manoharan, and he turned to look at her, mystified.

"Oh, dear sir, you are quite wrong there," said the nurse. "You are the father of a healthy baby girl, a carbon copy of her mother, I must say."

Dheeraj Manoharan's countenance changed from one of gladness to sheer horror. The nurse's words rang in his head like a Chinese gong: *a healthy baby girl . . . a healthy baby girl . . . a healthy baby girl.* Without saying a word, a dazed Dheeraj placed the newborn into

Shantaram's eager arms. Shantaram cooed at the baby, whispering foolish words to her while Mohan conveyed the gender of the baby to his father on the phone. When Shantaram held the baby out to Dheeraj, he rushed out of the ward, stunning all who had gathered there.

*

Dheeraj Manoharan never forgave Lord Shiva for not gifting him a son. The saddest part about the whole affair was that from the moment of the baby's birth, there was nothing but trouble for the mud blossom, Nirmala.

As Kesaribai cradled the infant in her arms in Nirmala's hospital room, Nirmala stared at the white-washed ceiling, waiting for her husband to come. Ameera Sheikh brought another beautiful bouquet of flowers for Nirmala, along with a box of toys.

"Neil sent all these for the little one," said Ameera, placing the gifts next to Nirmala's hospital bed. "Where is your husband? Busy at work?"

Nirmala didn't answer, but thanked Ameera and closed her eyes.

When Nirmala and her baby daughter returned home from the government hospital, Dheeraj Mano-haran was not there to greet them. His grandfather and her in-laws welcomed Nirmala home by performing an aarti at the front door before Nirmala entered the house. Dheeraj Manoharan returned home late that night. He did not even look at Nirmala or the baby. He simply ate the bread and butter Kesaribai made since Nirmala was nursing the baby.

After reciting the Hanuman Chalisa, Dheeraj Manoharan told his mother, "We are not going to spend money on bringing in a wet nurse for the newborn."

Kesaribai looked at him, astonished. "But . . . but we have to; otherwise, how will Nirmala be able to return to teaching once she is able to do so?"

Dheeraj Manoharan put up his hand and snarled loudly enough for Nirmala to hear him in the neighboring room.

"Tell Nirmala that she has to quit her job and look after the baby herself. I won't spend a rupee on a wet nurse for the sake of a girl-child."

"But the baby is your child, Dheeraj beta!" Kesaribai said. "How can you be angry with an innocent child?"

"And besides," a shocked Soham Manoharan said as he rose from his rocking chair, "it's hardly the baby's or the mother's fault that the child was born a girl. Take the child as a gift from the Goddess Lakshmi, the goddess of wealth and prosperity, and raise her up. The child's naming ceremony is coming soon, and all our relatives will be arriving for the ceremony. Don't create a scene."

"But Lord Shiva promised me a son!" Dheeraj Manoharan wailed, shaking his fists in the air.

"Maybe your next child will be a boy," said Soham Manoharan. "Stop being insensitive. Go to your wife and cradle the baby."

Dheeraj Manoharan trudged into the bedroom. Nirmala was seated on the bed with the baby girl on her lap. Dheeraj Manoharan pretended not to see Nirmala's red, swollen eyes. He picked up the baby and cradled her, the voice of his father echoing in his head. *Maybe your next child will be a boy.*

*

According to ancient customs and traditions of India, when a boy is born to a household, he brings with him happiness, the continuation of the family name, money to the family when he is old enough to work, a dowry from his wife, and pride to his mother for producing a son. A daughter, on the other hand, brings sadness, a state worse than barrenness, fear of rape, fear of pregnancy before marriage, dowry debts, bride burning, and possible widowhood. Dheeraj Manoharan, being a true son of the soil, felt the pinch when his daughter was born.

The girl had a naming ceremony, during which a young female cousin named her Kamala, which means *lotus.* Nirmala grew quiet after the birth of her daughter, for she realized that she had lost the favor of her husband. Dheeraj Manoharan was, however, determined to beget a son. After all, Lord Shiva had promised him, and he was going to make sure that his promise was kept.

He forced Nirmala to leave her job as a preschool teacher in order to look after Kamala. Kesaribai tried to reason with her son with her rudraksha in her right hand, but he ignored her words of wisdom. Dheeraj's father also brought Tarabai into the picture, but her son-in-law refused to meet with her.

"A fine mess her daughter has put me in. Gave me a daughter when I was hoping for a son. What can a daughter give to a lower-middle-class family but worry and tension?"

Through it all, Nirmala said nothing. She cared for her baby and remembered the times in her past when she played in the garbage with her urchin friends. She wondered where they were now. Had their parents sent them to school? She hoped their parents had been prudent and had not done so, for now it was obvious to Nirmala that education was a curse. It promised one so much that it diverted one's mind from brutal realities.

The next year, another child was born to Nirmala—another daughter. This time, Dheeraj Manoharan screamed and shouted and refused to be present at the naming ceremony. The girl was named Chandani, which means *the rays of the moon*. Nirmala nursed both of her daughters in silence. Ameera Sheikh and Neil Perez had, by this time, finished their graduation. They both came to Nirmala's in-laws place wearing their graduation robes. When they knocked at the door, however, Dheeraj Manoharan was at home. He opened the door, and seeing their faces, his blood boiled.

"What do you want?" he asked.

Ameera Sheikh hesitated, taken aback by Dheeraj's behavior. "We . . . we came to see Nirmala and her little ones."

"My wife is not at home. She has gone to buy the vegetables, and she has taken the children with her." And with that, he shut the door in their faces. Nirmala, who was home massaging Chandani at that time, shed silent tears that dripped from her cheeks and mixed with the massage oil on her baby's tender skin. Dheeraj Manoharan did not spare his wife.

The following year, the third daughter was born to Dheeraj Manoharan and Nirmala. She was named Gori, which meant *fairness*, as she was fair-complexioned like her father. After the naming ceremony, Kesaribai caught up with her son, who was sulking in the bedroom as he rocked Chandani in her cradle.

"Enough is enough, beta. Now we have three grandchildren; our family is complete. Let Nirmala go back to her job, and grandfather and I will care for the three girls."

Dheeraj Manoharan pretended not to hear his mother. He rose from the bed, put on a new kurta, and left the house.

*

That night, Dheeraj Manoharan ate dinner outside at a local restaurant in Dharavi. He was seated alone at his customary table drinking a cup of cold tea, when he felt a hand on his shoulder. He turned back and smiled.

"Hey, Ashutosh! I've not seen you for a long while. How are you?"

The young man sat down opposite him. Ashutosh was an old office friend who had left the job to start his own business in Vasai. Ashutosh smiled at Dheeraj as he ordered the waiter to bring another cup of tea. As they sipped their tea, the men discussed the days when they worked at the Tata Office as consultants.

"Hey, I almost forgot. Congratulations on the birth of your three baby girls," Ashutosh said. "Are you hoping for a son now, or you satisfied with the three goddesses in your house?"

Dheeraj Manoharan's face fell, and Ashutosh recognized the sadness in his friend's eyes. He tried to comfort Dheeraj.

"Okay, bhai, now I understand. Your heart yearns for a son, but you have tried three times, and all three times it's been a girl." Dheeraj nodded but said nothing. "My dear old colleague, you are too god-fearing. You've only been praying for a son and have not taken any steps to ensure that you will get one."

"How can one ensure a son?" muttered Dheeraj. "It's a gift from Prabhu. Maybe the burden of three girls is written for me."

"No, no my dear colleague. You are a graduate. Don't you know that there are clinical methods to detect whether you are going to get a son or daughter?"

Dheeraj stared in horror at Ashutosh. "Are you crazy? Sex detection tests are illegal. If ever I'm caught, I'll be jailed!"

"If you are caught, my dear colleague. *If!*"

Dheeraj shivered in his seat. He called to the waiter and asked him to serve cold water. When the water came, Dheeraj attacked it with a vigor that made Ashutosh grin."

"You are still the extra-cautious and god-fearing Dheeraj of the past, my dear colleague. With such an attitude, how will you ever get a son?"

Dheeraj wiped the sweat off his forehead and guzzled the icy water with a terrified but eager expression on his face. Ashutosh ordered another cup of tea for himself.

"I know a clinic in Vasai that conducts sex detection tests and abortions whenever necessary. Take my cell number. When the time comes, give me a call and I'll acquaint you with Dr. Srivastava, the head of the clinic."

Dheeraj stopped mopping his perspiring forehead and stared into his friend's eyes. He fidgeted with his fingers and asked himself whether he was that desperate for a son. Kamala, Chandni, and Gori were beautiful girls, but they would one day have to get married. Where would their dowries come from? How would he afford to conduct their marriages on a grand scale? If only he had a son to bring in a huge dowry from his wife's house. Then maybe . . .

"What are you thinking about, my dear colleague?" Ashutosh smiled and sipped his tea. "Don't worry. Dr. Srivastava is a known man to me. I had my sister-in-law's sex detection test done there. No sweat. And when we knew it was a girl, he aborted the child."

"Uh . . . aborted?" Dheeraj Manoharan could barely speak as he pictured his daughters being cut to bits by an evil-looking doctor in scrubs.

"Yes, aborted, of course. You don't expect the fetus to vanish into thin air, do you? Mind you, the abortion is done under wraps; no one will find out."

Ashutosh ordered the waiter to bring him a piece of paper, where he wrote down his new mobile number and handed it to Dheeraj Manoharan.

"When the time comes, don't forget my good advice. I'll go now. Got to get home early for some work. Give my greetings to your wife. Good evening to you, dear colleague." And with that, Ashutosh left the restaurant as Dheeraj Manoharan looked on, his face awash in awe and fear.

*

That night, Nirmala was rocking Chandani to sleep in her cradle. Kamala sat at her feet in the bedroom, playing with her favorite soft toys: a pink teddy bear and a brown horse.

"Mama-Mama-Mama," said two-year-old Kamala.

"What is it, lotus flower?" Nirmala cooed lovingly.

"Teddy bear! Teddy bear!"

"Yes, I know. The teddy bear is kissing the horse. Now play quietly, my precious lotus flower, while I put your sister to sleep."

"Sleep, Mama," Kamala said as she patted the bed. Nirmala laughed.

"Yes, yes. I'll put you to sleep, too, but only after I feed Gori her milk, okay?"

Kamala nodded her oiled and plaited head and continued to play with her stuffed toys. Nirmala rocked Chandani to sleep, trying hard to hold back the coughing fit that threatened to erupt. Three pregnancies without a break had taken a toll on Nirmala's body, especially her chest. She often felt short of breath, and though she'd told her husband about it, he ignored her and remained aloof.

A tear rolled down Nirmala's cheek as her husband came to mind. It was obvious even to outsiders that he longed for a son and was not satisfied with three angelic daughters.

Nirmala walked across the room and stared out the window. They stayed on the third floor, so Nirmala could get a good view of the Dharavi slum. She smiled as she saw a naked little boy playing in a nearby gutter without a care in the world, his body soaked in the filth of the city. Nirmala coughed again. Another tear rolled down her face when she glimpsed a teenage girl studying from a municipal schoolbook with the aid of a nearby streetlight. What memories that evoked in her!

Nirmala watched a procession of Shvetambara Jains as they walked barefoot through the Dharavi slum. Their mouths were covered with white cloth so no germs or any other tiny living creature would enter their mouths and die. They used brooms to sweep the path upon which they walked, so as not to trample on any living creature, and they walked barefoot so that if by chance they did walk over a stray ant, their body weight wouldn't kill the animal.

Nirmala longed to call out to those Jain pilgrims and leave everything behind to follow them in their never-ending journey toward moksha—salvation.

"Mama-Mama-Mama!"

Kamala's sweet voice brought Nirmala back to earth. She turned around, wiping her tears and smiling as she stared at her daughter.

"You are my good lotus flower. Keep this goodness within you, and Lord Vishnu will bless you, my darling."

Happy that her mother had smiled at her, Kamala returned to the courtship of the pink teddy bear and the brown horse. Looking at her, Nirmala promised herself that she would give her three girls the best education possible. She would not send them to a municipal school, but to a local convent school. Her mother-in-law had promised her that she would be able to look for another job after Gori was weaned. Kesaribai and the patriarch great-grandfather would look after the girls while Nirmala was out.

Nirmala coughed again, and Chandani awakened with a cry. Nirmala tied her saree pallu at her waist and hurried to the cradle to rock Chandani back to sleep.

"Hush little moonbeam, hush. Your father will get angry if he finds you making a noise at this time of night," Nirmala whispered.

When Dheeraj Manoharan returned home and entered the bedroom, he found Nirmala fast asleep on the bed, Gori on her left and Kamala on her right. Chandani slept peacefully in the wooden cradle. He also saw newly formed wrinkles at the sides of his wife's eyes, tiny feather strokes on her smooth, dark skin. Nirmala coughed softly in her sleep, but that didn't arouse her husband's sympathy at all. He stepped out of the room and entered the hall, where Kesaribai was seated cross-legged before the image of the god Shiva, praying with her eyes closed. Soham Manoharan was fast asleep on a mattress on the floor, the patriarch snoring loudly beside him.

Dheeraj Manoharan tapped his mother's shoulder.

"Oh beta, you have come at last. I hope you had a good dinner at the restaurant?"

"Yes, Ma, I did."

"Good, now go to bed. Nirmala is already asleep, and I hope now your craving for a son has ended. I am blissfully happy with Kamala, Chandani, and Gori. I've got big dreams for them."

Dheeraj Manoharan said nothing. He returned to the bedroom, changed into his pajamas, and lay beside Nirmala on the bed, hoping her vigorous coughing wouldn't keep him awake.

*

"You demon! I'll beat you till you're black-and-blue!" Dheeraj yelled as he hammered Nirmala with a wooden slipper while his family tried in vain to stop him. It was two years after the birth of Gori, and during that time, Nirmala had undergone four abortions. Each time she became pregnant, her husband and Ashutosh dragged her to the Vasai clinic. Each time it was a girl—and her husband gave orders for an abortion to be conducted. Nirmala always pleaded for mercy, but her husband beat her in front of her in-laws and innocent children instead.

"You witch," Dheeraj screamed, "you can't even give me a son! Your womb is cursed! Do you hear me? Cursed!" Nirmala winced as he kicked her in the stomach. Thin and weak after a string of pregnancies and abortions, Nirmala coughed like a hound from hell as the wooden slipper fell like lightning upon her, bruising her and cutting her flesh. Kamala, four years old and in tears, tried to push her father off her mother, but was pulled to safety by Kesaribai. Chandani covered Gori's eyes as both girls huddled in the corner of their tiny home, trying not to watch the gory spectacle.

Mud blossom. Mud blossom. The voice of Nirmala's mother echoed in her ears as the wooden slipper came down on her head, cutting it open. Bright red blood fell upon Nirmala's saree and neck, making Kesaribai scream and Soham gasp as they tried to pull their son off their daughter-in-law.

"You fool! It will be a police case. Stop hitting her this instant!" Soham yelled, before his son rudely pushed him away. Wild with rage and blind with anger, Dheeraj dropped the slipper . . . and picked up the matchbox from the hall table.

"I will teach this cursed witch a lesson: I will burn her to death!"

With that, Dheeraj—the once shy man and observer of religious practices, now blind and obsessed with the desire for a son—set the saree of Nirmala on fire.

"Mama-Mama-Mama," wailed Kamala.

"Quick, Kamala beti! Get a thick bedsheet from the bedroom!" Kesaribai yelled as she hit her son and yanked the matchbox from his hand. The great-grand-father watched aghast as the flames traveled toward Nirmala's breast. Concerned neighbors and slum dwellers pounded on the door, yelling that domestic violence was a crime and that they would call the police. Kesaribai picked up a chair and swung it at her son, knocking him out. She used her own hands to put out the flames that consumed her daughter-in-law, getting burnt in the process. At last, Kamala brought the bedsheet and Soham wrapped his daughter-in-law in it, subduing the flames. Nirmala was saved, but suffered horrible burns on her hands, stomach, and legs.

"Fire! Fire!" yelled the slum dwellers. Unable to control the crowd outside his door any longer, Soham opened the door. When the neighbors barged into the room, they gasped. Dheeraj was sprawled unconscious on the floor, while Nirmala lay whimpering next to him—burnt, bleeding, and in terrible pain. With the help of the neighbors, Nirmala was rushed to the hospital.

*

Mud blossom. Mud blossom.

Nirmala was dreaming and she knew it. She saw herself studying at night under the street lamp in the Reclamation slum and heard her mother, Tarabai, call out to her: Mud blossom . . . mud blossom. She saw Shantaram clicking away at his computer with a smile on his thin face. Naked street urchins chased the chickens past his shanty, and there was Nirmala, right up in front, smiling and hitting the chickens with a stick.

Nirmala bachchee, you have scored a distinction. Mud blossom of our slum . . . mud blossom.

Then Nirmala heard a whip—the whip of a belt. Her mother was belting her. Hard. What had she done? Oh yes, she could not produce a son. Wasn't that the reason Tarabai belted her? Somehow, something seemed wrong with that analysis. Maybe she was going mad and needed to see the school nurse. She would have to make the school nurse promise not to say a word about this to her mother. But why the secrecy? Was it because she smelt of human excreta?

Mud blossom . . . mud blossom.

Amina. Where was Amina, her childhood friend? Oh yes! She was still making the mutton for her Abbujaan, as he was at home today. But Nirmala wanted her to come outside to chase the chickens in the mud. Nirmala tried to grab Amina's hand but as she touched her,

Amina crumbled into sawdust. All that remained in Nirmala's hand was Amina's black burka.

Mud blossom. Mud blossom, are you awake dear?

No, Nirmala was not awake. How could she be awake? She was still in her mother's womb . . . but she was just a fetus. She was a female fetus. No! That wouldn't do; her husband wanted a son. So he and Ashutosh would have to take her to that clinic in Vasai and abort her. Wait! That didn't make sense either, for where would they dump her? Oh yes! Of course. In the dustbin . . . and then she would be known as mud blossom, a beautiful dark flower from the mud.

Why can't she hear us? Mud blossom! Mud blossom, please get up!

No, she could not get up yet; the college lecture was still going on. Neil Perez was sitting to her right, smiling, while Ameera Sheikh was sitting to her left.

You must finish your graduation, Nirmala, mud blossom.

But Nirmala had promised her mother that she would only finish her twelfth-grade. Graduation was out of the question. But she would make Kamala a doctor, Chandani a lawyer, and Gori a teacher. But why was she thinking of girl children again? Her husband wanted a son.

"Nirmala Manoharan, are you awake now?"

As Nirmala opened her eyes, the dream faded into the background. A doctor's face loomed above her; behind him, a nurse looked on with a concerned expression on her face. Nirmala tried to lift herself up, but the doctor wouldn't allow it.

"Lie down, dear; you've got too many bruises, wounds, and burns to get up now. Your whole family is outside waiting for you."

In a flash, Nirmala remembered the events of the night. Her husband had beaten her up and had burnt her; apparently she had survived. She looked up at the doctor and raised her hand to his.

"Doctor, call Kamala, my eldest daughter, in here."

"I'm sorry, Mrs. Manoharan, but none of your children are here in the hospital. Apparently, they are staying with your neighbors for the night."

"Call my mother-in-law, then."

"Certainly. But first . . . Mrs. Manoharan?"

"Yes?"

"There is . . . there is a policeman waiting to see you, about the wounds and the burning. Just routine. Tell him the truth and don't panic, all right?"

It took a minute for the doctor's words to register. Nirmala nodded.

"Good! Then I will send in your mother-in-law and the police constable at once. Your mother-in-law and nurse Audrey will be your witnesses." And with that, the doctor left the hospital room.

The police constable entered along with Kesaribai. The frenzied mother-in-law ran toward Nirmala, grabbed her right hand, and sobbed into it. However, Nirmala's attention was not on Kesaribai but on the constable. The man dressed in khaki stood with a register and a pen in his hand.

"Mrs. Nirmala Dheeraj Manoharan, I'm here to question you about the night of June eighth, last night."

"Yes, constable, what about it?"

"How did you get these terrible wounds, including the burns on your arms, stomach, and legs, and the gash on your head?"

Kesaribai, a pleading look upon her pathetic face, shook her head, encouraging Nirmala not to say anything. Nirmala was in no mood to play the dutiful daughter-in-law. She coughed a time or two, then spoke with a stern voice.

"It was my husband who beat me up with a wooden slipper and then burned my saree."

"Who was present when your husband was attacking you?"

Kesaribai wept, turning away from Nirmala and burying her face in the end of her saree. Nirmala continued, unfazed.

"When my husband was attacking me, my grandfather-in-law, my father-in-law Soham Manoharan, my mother-in-law Kesaribai, and my three children—Kamala, Chandani and Gori—were present."

"Did any of them try to stop your husband?"

"Yes. Everyone tried, but he was in a mad frenzy."

"What for?"

"Day before yesterday was my fifth abortion. I've not been able to provide him with a boy child, so he has been beating me for quite a while now."

"Where was this abortion conducted?"

"At the Good Health Clinic in Vasai."

"What is the name of the doctor who conducted it?"

"Doctor Srivastava. He conducted all my abortions."

Kesaribai listened in horror as Nirmala gave detail after detail of the tortures to which she'd been subjected. Something inside her still pleaded for support of her son's cause, but when she was made to sign the constable's register, she did so with a shaking hand.

The constable shut his register. "So you want to file a case against your husband, right?"

"Yes, constable," replied Nirmala, no trace of doubt in her voice.

"Good. What you have told me explains everything, including the state of your present predicament. I'm sorry this happened to you, Mrs. Manoharan, but such disreputable clinics are known to have cases such as these."

"What . . . what cases?"

The constable looked shocked. "Why, um . . . didn't the doctor tell you?"

"Tell me what?"

The constable looked at the nurse, then at the quizzical face of Kesaribai before replying.

"Why, my lady, because of going to an unsanitary clinic, you have contracted the HIV virus. You are now HIV positive!"

*

Many people in India die from AIDS every single day. When Nirmala heard that she was HIV positive, she wailed and wept her heart out; medically, there is no stigma in India as great as the stigma of the HIV virus—which ultimately leads to AIDS . . . and then death.

Hearing the news about Nirmala's disease, Kesaribai beat her chest and cursed her destiny and ill luck. Dheeraj Manoharan was tested for AIDS before he was jailed—he was clear. Then the three girls were tested. They, too, were clear. The testing was expensive, but Kesaribai insisted it be done. Soham Manoharan paid for the tests from his own salary, his heart bleeding in pain for his grandchildren.

Nirmala was discharged from the hospital after a week.

"Mama-Mama-Mama." Kamala's voice echoed in the ears of the dazed Nirmala. At first Nirmala gave into despair, but looking at her three children gave her courage to go on with her life—AIDS or no AIDS. But the atmosphere in the house on the third floor overlooking Dharavi had changed. Kesaribai's heart hardened toward Nirmala, as she was the cause of her only son being in jail. She also forbade Nirmala from entering the kitchen and from cooking anything.

"Who can tell?" Nirmala heard Kesaribai tell her husband. "She may give her disease to all of us. It is dangerous to house such an unclean creature."

All the family members conspired to keep the three girls away from Nirmala. Soham Manoharan instructed Nirmala not to bathe in the family toilet but in the municipal toilet downstairs on the outskirts of Dharavi. Food was served sparingly to Nirmala on a separate plate, and Kesaribai forbade Nirmala from performing puja—prayers—to the statute of Lord Shiva.

"It is bad enough that she has brought this curse into our house; she will pollute Lord Shiva with her presence," Kesaribai said while cooking vegetable soup in the kitchen.

Nirmala bore all of it with patience because she knew her family members were ignorant about the disease.

One day, Nirmala was seated on the floor opposite Kesaribai, watching as the woman massaged Gori with oil.

"Ma, please may I hold the child for a moment?"

Kesaribai ignored her and continued to massage the child.

Nirmala couldn't contain her tears. "I . . . I've not touched the child for weeks. Please, may I just hold her for a moment?"

"Not on your life, ashubh aurat," yelled Kesaribai. "Just because we are giving you shelter under our roof does not mean you can order me about. Never will I allow you to touch the children. Never!"

Kesaribai twitched her nose and continued to massage her granddaughter. When Soham Manoharan entered the house after work and asked Kesaribai for a cup of coffee, Nirmala immediately brightened up.

"Babuji, I'll make it for you."

"No way!" Kesaribai yelled so loudly that Gori began to cry. "No way will you make anything for my dear husband with your cursed hands. This is the punishment that one receives for betraying one's husband to the police."

Nirmala sat in silence, her muscles twitching in shock as she watched Kesaribai hand Gori to Soham, before washing her hands and making her husband a cup of coffee.

The great-grandfather of the house was seated near the window with a pail of water and a mop at his side. He had this unusual idea in his head that the house had to repeatedly be cleaned so Nirmala's disease wouldn't spread to the rest of the family. Every hour, he would move from his seat to mop the floor of the hall or the bedroom, mumbling to himself.

"Karma. It is all Karma."

When dinnertime came, everyone gathered at the dining table except Nirmala, who remained in her place on the floor with her plate at her feet, isolated from the rest of the family.

"Dadima, why is Mother not allowed to touch us?" Kamala asked her grandmother. She stared at her poor mother, who was nibbling the food she was served with tears running down her cheeks.

"Your mother sent your father to jail. She is a bad woman; as a punishment, she contracted a terrible, cursed disease. I don't want you girls to catch her dirty disease, so I make sure she doesn't touch you," said Kesaribai. The ignorant Kamala nodded her head and looked toward Nirmala.

"You are bad, Mama. Very, very bad."

Hearing these words from her elder sister, Chandani also took up the heartbreaking chant.

It was all Nirmala could take, and she wept in despair. She put her plate on the floor and cried into the end of her saree until it became a sodden pulp.

After finishing his dinner, her husband's great-grandfather washed his hands, picked up his pail of water and mop, and started cleaning the house for the tenth time that day. As he came near Nirmala he growled.

"Get up, you disobedient wife. I have to clean that spot where you are sitting, you unclean wretch!"

Then Nirmala saw red. She snatched the mop from the patriarch's hands and whipped herself, opening up her wounds, dripping her infected blood onto the floor.

"Bad mother. Bad mother," Kamala and Chandani cried as they watched their mother hit herself.

"Somebody stop her!" The patriarch watched in dismay as Nirmala's tainted blood spattered over the wall and the floor.

Nirmala, however, was in a rage and felt self-mortification was the best way to rid her heart of the pain built up inside.

"Bad mother! Bad mother! Bad mother!"

"Somebody stop her! Somebody stop her!"

Nirmala dropped the mop and picked up a belt Soham Manoharan had left on a nearby sofa. She inflicted blow after blow to her battered body.

"Bad mother! Bad mother! Bad mother!"

Kesaribai grabbed Nirmala's hands, but was pushed away.

Mud blossom. Mud blossom.

"Bad mother! Bad mother! Bad mother!"

Nirmala continued to belt herself. The wound on her head opened, and bright red blood drenched the snow-white blouse of her saree. The patriarch was berserk, darting about the house trying in vain to swab up the blood that was spreading all over the hall and splattering his own face and the faces of his grandchildren.

"Bad mother! Bad mother! Bad mother!"

Nirmala bachchee, you've got a distinction in the tenth-grade board exams! A distinction!

The belt buckle tore Nirmala's blouse as she whipped her breasts. Kesaribai again tried to get hold of her but was tossed away. As Soham struggled to wrestle the belt from Nirmala's hands, the neighbors pounded on the door.

"Bad mother! Bad mother! Bad mother!"

I can't come out to play now, Nirmala. I have to knead the dough. Abbujaan is at home today.

Nirmala's white saree was drenched in blood. As one of the elderly neighbors threatened to break down the door, Kesaribai grabbed Nirmala's feet in an attempt to drop her to the ground. Nirmala kicked Kesaribai away and continued to whip herself, though she was growing tired with every movement she made.

"Bad mother! Bad mother! Bad mother!"

Nirmala, think of your future. Complete your graduation. And you can't deny it, Neil likes you . . . Neil really likes you . . .

Kesaribai wailed as Nirmala continued to belt herself. The patriarch gave up on cleaning and carried the three children to the bedroom. At last, Soham Manoharan grabbed the belt from Nirmala's hand and slapped her hard across the face. The neighbors broke down the door, and one of the younger women shrieked at the sight of all the blood splashed across the walls and furniture. Someone lifted Soham off Nirmala, who was lying on the floor screaming in pain.

Bad mother! Bad mother! Bad mother!

You witch, you can't even give me a son! I want a son . . . a son . . . a son!

Nirmala jumped up, pushed all the neighbors aside, and ran barefoot and bleeding from the building.

"Stop her! Somebody stop her!" Kesaribai screamed and beat her chest and her head as she lay on the floor. Nirmala ran away, into the night, her blood-soaked hair left loose and matted to her battered face. She ran like the shot of a gun. Many of the Dharavi residents stared at her, but no one interfered.

*

An angry Tarabai stood outside her hut with her hands on her hips. Nirmala stood before her, out of breath and panting from running all the way from Dharavi to the Bandra Reclamation Area. Tarabai stared disapprovingly at Nirmala's bloody wounds, bloodstained saree, and angry face.

"You should not have come here, mud blossom." Tarabai's stern voice sent a chill down Nirmala's spine. Shantaram and Amina's father were also present outside the hut of Tarabai. After hearing that Nirmala had AIDS, Shantaram did not step forward to touch her, nor did Amina's father, who called for the local witch doctor to come to Tarabai's hut to bandage Nirmala's wounds.

The witch doctor came with a cauldron of warm water and used a mug to pour the water upon Nirmala, washing her wounds—especially the one on the back of her head. Tarabai made sure none of her sons came out of the hut to see their sister in such a state.

"You should go back, Nirmala," Tarabai said. "This is no longer your home, and I won't have an AIDS patient in my hut."

Shantaram handed a towel to the witch doctor, who blotted her wounds with a gentle hand.

"They treated me like an animal at Dharavi! They acted like it's my fault that I've got AIDS, when it was all my husband's fault. They isolated me from my three daughters and made me sit in one corner of the house. Please, Ma, let me stay here with you. I'll serve you like a servant for the rest of my life."

Shantaram's heart melted, and he turned toward Tarabai and said, "Let her stay here with us, Tarabai. Maybe it is God's will."

"I have neither the money nor the patience to look after an AIDS patient. Do you have any clue what a stain Nirmala's disease will be on my family?" Tarabai cried in rage. "No one will marry my three sons because of this bloody witch and her incurable disease. Besides, do you know how expensive the medicines will be? No! She can't stay here with us."

Nirmala stared at her mother as the witch doctor poured pail after pail of water on her and wiped her wounds. Many thoughts passed through Nirmala's mind at that point—including thoughts of suicide.

That night, Nirmala sat on a pile of garbage near the Bandra Reclamation slum. The bacteria and germs crawled into her body, but she didn't care. A stray dog sat beside her, licking the bloody wound on Nirmala's arm. Thoughts about her life passed before her eyes like pictures across a cinema screen: her childhood, her college days, her marriage, her daughters, the abortions, AIDS. And now? What next, Nirmala?

The stray dog continued to lick the blood from Nirmala's arm, but when the wound went dry, the dog bit her. Nirmala's screams sent the dog running.

"Get away from me! Get away!"

In the early hours of the morning, Nirmala, reeking of blood and the stench of garbage, walked toward the beach. She had begun to feel a tremendous pain in her bones that dimmed the light within her eyes; all she saw now was the one option left for her . . . the option of death. At last she would be away from all her persecutors and enemies. Her children didn't need her, her in-laws hated her, her husband despised her, and her mother didn't want her. But the Arabian Sea—the sea of the Arab—was opening its arms in the distance, welcoming her into its watery embrace. A thin smile spread across Nirmala's cracked lips. No more thinking, no more worrying, no more anxiety, no more dreams. Death. Just death . . . the companion of the afflicted.

Nirmala edged her way toward the water and tested it with her toes. The icy cold water chilled her bones, but Nirmala was determined. She headed into the water, not stopping until it reached her waist. As the water lapped around her, Nirmala smiled. At last, true peace was at hand. She took a deep breath and let the stray thoughts flow from her mind: Where was Amina? Was she married and kneading the dough in someone else's house? Had Ameera and Neil finished their graduation? Post-graduation? Did Neil still like her? Would he send orchids to her funeral? She had grown quite fond of blue orchids. How was her husband doing in jail? When would he be released? What was Kamala doing this morning? Who would oil her hair? Would she be allowed to come to her mother's funeral?

Nirmala slipped into deeper water and shivered as it caressed her breasts. Would Chandani and Gori even remember that they had a mother? Would Tarabai feel guilty if she were to see the drowned body of the daughter she'd always despised? Was Dr. Srivastava conducting another abortion in Vasai today? What would her in-laws do with her things? Burn them? What will they do when they find an empty syringe in an old geometry box lying somewhere under the bed?

Nirmala lifted her hands toward the heavens, and after asking for forgiveness to the almighty Lord Brahma who created her, she ducked under the waters.

*

"Nirmala! Nirmala, wake up!"

Nirmala opened her eyes and, to her surprise, found Neil bending over her.

"Is this another sweet dream?" muttered Nirmala, her wounds and lips raw and painful.

"No dream, idiot," Neil said. "I was here on the beach clicking some photographs for my boss when I saw you duck under the water."

Nirmala then realized that her body lay on the sand, her head in Neil's drenched lap. She looked up at Neil with a troubled expression on her face.

"You should have left me to die."

"Why?"

"Because I have AIDS, Neil, and no one wants me."

"I want you, Nirmala."

Nirmala smiled weakly. "I won't last much longer."

"I'll be with you for as long as I can have you, dear."

Nirmala looked into Neil's light brown eyes and saw the sunshine flow from them like a warm embrace. She lifted her limp right hand and touched Neil's cheek. He turned his head and brushed his lips across her palm.

"Aren't you afraid to kiss me? After all, I have AIDS."

To that, Neil bent down and kissed Nirmala's tattered gray lips. It was a long kiss which brought warmth to Nirmala's otherwise cold and shivering body. After Neil lifted his head and put his right hand on her forehead, Nirmala smiled.

"May the Lord Vishnu shower you with all his blessings."

"I would rather have you and your dreams than Lord Vishnu's blessings, Nirmala," Neil whispered.

Nirmala tried to answer, but a fit of coughing overtook her, rattling her bones and sending a trickle of blood from the corner of her withered mouth. And still she smiled.

"I entrust to you all my good wishes and dreams. Thank you for letting me die at your feet rather than in the sea." And with that, Nirmala closed her eyes on the world.

Mud blossom. Mud blossom.

***

FORTHCOMING TITLE

Amina: The Silent One
by Fiza Pathan

Synopsis:

Amina: The Silent One is the story of a musical prodigy born in the slums of Mumbai and her journey into hell. Born to Jaffer and his wife, Amina is their third female child, and they want to get rid of her. But sage advice from a professor of history changes their minds. This is the story about how poverty, sexual debasement, and sexual abuse is meted out to Amina, and how music can sometimes melt a heart of stone. Can Amina overcome the poverty she's been born into, her second-class status as a woman, and the sexual abuse she is made to withstand? Or will she sink into anonymity? This novella will get under your skin and stay with you for years to come.

Review Quotes:

"Fast-paced and intense, this book is well plotted and will keep readers turning pages."—*The Booklife Prize*

"A powerfully gripping tale told by Fiza Pathan, *Amina: The Silent One* will fire up reader's emotions while bringing them to tears."—*Authors Talk About It*

"A truly remarkable work of fiction that touches heart and mind, *Amina: The Silent One* is sure to engender much thought and discussion. It is recommended without reservation."—*Book Viral*

"*Amina: The Silent One* by Fiza Pathan is one of the most socially relevant books on the market today in my opinion, and I highly recommend it. I could not put this book down. I was totally captivated throughout the entire story, and Amina and her family will be in my head, and on my heart for some time to come."—*Reader Views*

"Pathan paints a visceral image of slum life, and her likeable protagonist Amina helps to draw a reader in who might otherwise be ignorant to such an experience. The beautiful novel is an important read thanks to the issues it illustrates that so many women face not just in India, but in other parts of the world as well."— "6 Titles to Help Diversify Your Reads" by Joe Sutton for *IndieReader*

Awards:

2015-2016 Reader Views Literary Awards - Global Award for Asia
2015-2016 Reader Views Literary Awards - Winner 1st Place General Fiction/Novel
2016 Readers' Favorite International Book Award - Bronze Medal
Foreword Reviews' 2015 INDIEFAB Book of the Year Award -Finalist Multicultural (Adult Fiction)

2015 New Apple Book Awards - Medalist Winner in the eBook General Fiction

2016 Next Generation Indie Book Awards - Finalist Novella Category

4th Annual Beverly Hills International Book Awards – Winner in Regional Fiction

2016 IAN Book of the Year Awards - Finalist General Fiction

2016 IAN Book of the Year Awards - Finalist Novella

Shortlisted in the 2016 Book Viral Book Awards

55 Best Self-Published Books of 2015 – IndieReader

2015 Pinnacle Book Achievement Award - Category Fiction

2015 New England Book Festival - Honorable Mention in Regional Literature

2016 Pacific Rim Book Festival - RUNNER-UP Regional Literature.

2016 Hollywood Book Festival - Honorable Mention (Wild Card entry)

2016 Great Midwest Book Festival - Runner-Up in Regional Literature

ABOUT THE AUTHOR

Fiza Pathan has a bachelor's degree in arts from the University of Mumbai, where she majored in history and sociology with a first class. She also has a bachelor's degree in education, again with a first class, her special subjects being English and history.

Fiza has written eleven award-winning books and a short story, "Flesh of Flesh," which reflect her interest in furthering the cause of education and in championing social issues. In over sixty literary competitions, she has placed either as winner or finalist, chief among them being: Readers' Favorite Book Awards; Reader Views Literary Awards; Eric Hoffer Book Award; Foreword Reviews Indie Fab Book Awards; Mom's Choice Awards; Literary Classics Book Awards; and Dan Poynter's Global Ebook Awards. She lives with her maternal family and writes novels and short stories in most genres. You may follow her on Twitter @FizaPathan and subscribe to her blog http://insaneowl.wordpress.com/feed/ You can learn more about her at the link below: https://margaretjeanlangstaff.com/2016/01/02/love-is-the-slowest-form-of-suicide-fiza-pathan/

Amazon link: http://www.amazon.com/Fiza-Pathan/e/B0091BCNTU

Website: http://fizapathanpublishing.ink/